ChangelingPress.com

Salvation (Reckless Kings MC 5)

A Dixie Reapers Bad Boys Romance

Harley Wylde

Salvation (Reckless Kings MC 5)
A Dixie Reapers Bad Boys Romance
Harley Wylde

ISBN: 978-1-60521-964-6

Publisher:
Changeling Press LLC
315 N. Centre St.
Martinsburg, WV 25404
ChangelingPress.com

Printed in the U.S.A.

Editor: Crystal Esau
Cover Artist: Bryan Keller

The individual stories in this anthology have been previously released in E-Book format.

Table of Contents

Salvation (Reckless Kings MC 5)
A Dixie Reapers Bad Boys Romance
Harley Wylde

Is it friendship or something more? I think I'm ready to find out.

Yulia -- They call him Salvation, and that's exactly what he's been for me. I was only sixteen when he swept me up into his arms and carried me out of hell. Things were so bad, all I wanted was to die. He and his club, the Reckless Kings, they saved me. Salvation's never touched me, even though we're technically married, and he honestly has enough on his plate already with a daughter who's badly scarred from an explosion. But we've been together for eleven years now, and the older I get, the more I want our marriage to be real.

Salvation -- Since the day Yulia came to live with me, I've not once cheated on her. She's legally my wife, and that's all that matters. Besides, my daughter, Clover, has kept me busy. Now Clover's nearly an adult and I've noticed the way Yulia looks at me when she thinks I'm not paying attention. But can we have a real marriage when we've been nothing but friends all these years? It's too bad my family has be to taken before I realize the answer to that question. Now I'll do whatever it takes to get Clover and Yulia back, and I'll send their kidnappers straight to hell.

What Came Before...

In Forge's book, we discovered the club girls had their own set of problems they were trying to escape from. Whisper decided to help them. She gave Carina food for her girls and offered money for her rent. A Prospect named Kye had fallen for Carina and helped her and the girls as much as he could, but by the end of the book, someone had blown up Carina's RV, killing her and one of her daughters. Her second daughter, Clover, survived but was burned on her face and arms. Kye took in Clover as his own daughter, even though he was still a Prospect. The club gave them a house and helped them as much as they could.

There's also some crossover with the Dixie Reapers in Grimm's book. His woman, Oksana, has a sister -- Yulia -- the Bratva sent to a boarding school, where she was sexually assaulted and abused. The Reckless Kings are the closest and go in to save her. At the time, she's only sixteen, but it's decided one of them will marry her, on paper only, to keep her safe from the Bratva... Kye is the one who takes her in.

And this is where her story begins...

Prologue

Yulia

The wind whipped my hair across my face, stinging my eyes as I stood at the edge of the school grounds. My heart pounded, each beat a reminder of the choice before me. Memories flashed through my mind -- cruel hands, mocking laughter, endless fear. I closed my eyes, willing the images away.

This was it. The end. My fingers trembled as I gripped the knife tighter. Just one cut and it would all be over. No more pain. No more shame. I took a shaky breath. "*Prosti menya, sestra,*" I whispered. *Forgive me, sister.*

The blade glinted in the fading sunlight. So sharp. So final. I pressed it to my wrist.

A roar split the air.

My eyes snapped open. In the distance, a motorcycle engine growled, growing louder. Closer. I hesitated, the knife hovering above my skin. Who would come here? Why now? The engine's rumble filled my ears, drowning out the frantic beating of my heart. Despite myself, I turned toward the sound.

A flicker of… something. Not quite hope. But curiosity. A momentary distraction from the abyss. I lowered the knife, just slightly. My mind raced. Should I wait? See who it was? Or finish what I'd started?

The motorcycle drew nearer. Any moment now, it would crest the hill. I bit my lip, indecision paralyzing me. The wind continued to howl around me, urging me forward. But that sound… it called to me. Promising… what?

I didn't know.

For just a moment, my despair lifted. And in that moment, I chose to wait.

The motorcycle crested the hill, its rider a dark silhouette against the blazing orange sky. My breath caught in my throat. He was massive, all broad shoulders and muscled limbs, his leather cut emblazoned with a patch I couldn't quite make out.

He dismounted in one fluid motion, his boots hitting the ground with a heavy *thud*. My fingers tightened around the knife as he strode toward me, his pace urgent but measured. "Easy now, darlin'," he called out, his voice a low rumble that carried on the wind. "Why don't you put that knife down?"

I shook my head, taking a step back. "Stay away," I warned. "I don't know you."

He slowed his approach, hands raised placatingly. "Name's Hawk. I'm with the Reckless Kings. I was sent here to help. A few of my brothers are waiting nearby to make sure we don't run into trouble."

My mind reeled. *The Reckless Kings*? How did they know? Why would they care? "No one can help," I whispered, more to myself than to him. "It's too late."

Hawk took another careful step forward. "It's never too late, sweetheart. Trust me on that."

I laughed, a bitter sound that surprised even me. "*Trust*? I don't even know what that means anymore."

His gaze met mine. "Then let me show you. Just… put the knife down. Please."

My hand trembled. Part of me wanted to believe him, to grasp at this lifeline he was offering. But the fear, the pain of the past years, it all threatened to drown me. "I can't," I choked out. "You don't understand what he did to me."

Hawk's expression softened. "Maybe not exactly.

But I've seen enough pain in this world to recognize it. You're not alone, Yulia. Not anymore."

My name on his lips startled me. *How did he know? Who sent him*?

As if sensing my thoughts, he added, "Your sister's worried sick. She asked us to find you."

Tears welled in my eyes. "Oksana?"

Hawk nodded. "She loves you. Let us help. Let me take you somewhere safe."

The knife slipped in my grasp, my resolve wavering… The knife clattered to the ground, and my legs gave out. I crumpled, expecting to hit the cold earth. Instead, strong arms caught me, steadying me against a broad chest.

"I've got you," Hawk murmured, his voice a low rumble. "You're safe now."

I trembled, my body wracked with silent sobs. Years of pent-up fear and pain poured out of me as Hawk held me, his grip firm but gentle. "Can you walk?" he asked after a moment.

I nodded weakly, not trusting my voice. Hawk kept an arm around me as he guided me toward his motorcycle. The machine loomed before us, all gleaming chrome and sleek lines. "Ever ridden before?" Hawk asked, swinging his leg over the seat.

I shook my head, eyeing the bike warily. "*Nyet…* no."

He extended his hand. "First time for everything. Hold on tight, okay?"

With shaking fingers, I grasped his hand and climbed on behind him. The leather of his cut was smooth under my palms as I wrapped my arms around his waist. I heard three more motorcycles and noticed the men were also from the Reckless Kings.

"Ready?" Hawk called over his shoulder.

"Da," I whispered, tightening my grip.

The engine roared to life, vibrating through my entire body. We took off, the world blurring around us as we sped away from the school grounds. Away from my nightmares.

I pressed my face against Hawk's back, the wind whipping my hair. Part of me still couldn't believe this was real. That I was escaping. That someone had come for me. "Where are we going?" I shouted over the engine's rumble.

"Somewhere safe," Hawk called back. "Our compound. You'll be protected there."

Protected. The word sent a shiver through me -- of fear or hope, I wasn't sure.

As we rode into the gathering darkness, I clung to Hawk, to this stranger who'd become my unexpected savior. My mind raced with questions, with doubts. But for now, I let the roar of the engine drown out my thoughts, focusing only on the road ahead and the promise of safety it held.

Tears stung my eyes, instantly whisked away by the biting wind. My chest ached with each ragged breath, emotions churning like a storm inside me. Gratitude and terror warred for dominance.

"You okay back there?" Hawk's voice barely reached me over the engine's roar.

I nodded against his back, not trusting my voice. My fingers dug into the leather of his cut, anchoring me to this surreal moment.

The scenery blurred past -- trees, buildings, flashes of light. My mind struggled to process it all. What would happen to me now? Who were these men? Could I truly trust them? Even though he'd said Oksana sent them, maybe I shouldn't have trusted him. And yet, why else would he have known my name or where to find me?

Before I could spiral further, the bike slowed. We turned onto a gravel road, the change in terrain jolting me from my thoughts. Ahead, a large compound loomed, encircled by a high stone fence. As we approached, the gates swung open. The sudden cacophony of noise and activity hit me like a physical force.

Motorcycles revved. Men shouted greetings. Music blared from somewhere. The scent of gasoline and cigarette smoke filled the air. Hawk pulled to a stop, and I reluctantly loosened my death grip on him. My legs trembled as I dismounted, nearly buckling beneath me.

"Welcome to your new home, sweetheart," Hawk said, his voice gentler than I expected.

I blinked, overwhelmed by the sea of leather-clad figures surrounding us. Some eyed me curiously, others with open suspicion. "Who's the girl?" a gruff voice called out.

"None of your damn business," Hawk snapped back. He placed a protective hand on my shoulder, steering me toward a large building. "Let's get you inside."

I stumbled along, my heart pounding. "I… I don't understand," I whispered.

Hawk's grip tightened reassuringly. "You're safe now. That's all that matters for tonight."

As we entered the building, the noise faded. I took a shaky breath, trying to center myself in this strange new world.

A tall man with dark, tousled hair stepped forward from the shadowed interior. His presence commanded attention, but his eyes… they were unexpectedly gentle. "Yulia," he said softly, his voice a low rumble that sent an involuntary shiver down my spine. "I'm Kye."

I swallowed hard, my throat dry. "How do you know my name?"

He smiled, the expression warming his features. "We've been expecting you."

My heart stuttered. "You have?"

Kye nodded, his gaze never leaving mine. "You're safe here, Yulia. I promise you that."

Something in his tone, in the steadiness of his gaze, made me want to believe him. I felt the iron bands of fear around my chest loosen even more.

"Come," Kye said, gesturing toward a nearby room. "We need to talk."

I hesitated, glancing back at Hawk. He nodded encouragingly. "It's okay, sweetheart. Kye'll take good care of you."

Taking a deep breath, I followed Kye into what appeared to be an office. He closed the door behind us, the click seeming to echo in the sudden quiet. "Sit, please," he said, indicating a worn leather couch.

I perched on the edge, my body tense. Kye leaned against the desk, his posture relaxed but his eyes intent. "Yulia, there's something I need to explain to you," he began. "It's… unconventional, but it's the best way we can keep you safe."

My stomach clenched. "What is it?"

Kye took a breath. "We need to get married."

I blinked, certain I'd misheard. "Married? To… to you?"

He nodded, his expression serious. "It would be in name only, of course. But it would give you legal protection, make it harder for anyone to touch you."

My mind reeled. "But… why would you do that? You don't even know me."

Kye's eyes softened. "Because it's the right thing to do. And because I made a promise to keep you safe."

I stared at him, searching for any hint of deception. But all I saw was sincerity and a quiet strength that made me want to trust him, despite everything. "I… I don't know what to say," I whispered.

"The club is pretty much pushing for this, as in neither of us gets a say. I figure you've had enough people telling you what to do. So, between the two of us, I'm going to let you choose. You don't have to decide right now," Kye assured me. "But I want you to know that this offer comes with no strings attached. Your safety is my only concern."

I nodded slowly, my thoughts a tangled mess.

Kye's hand hovered near my elbow, not quite touching. "Let me show you to your room. But should you agree to the marriage, you'll move into my house. To be clear, you'll have your own room there too."

I followed him down a dim hallway, my footsteps echoing. The compound felt vast, a labyrinth of concrete and steel.

My new cage? Or my sanctuary?

We stopped at a heavy wooden door. Kye demonstrated the lock, his movements deliberate. "This is yours. No one enters without your permission. Not even me."

The door swung open. I stepped inside, heart pounding.

"How does it feel?" Kye's voice was gentle.

I surveyed the space -- simple furnishings, a small window. Clean. Safe. "It's… mine?" The word felt foreign on my tongue.

Kye nodded. "Entirely. You're free here, Yulia."

Free. The concept dizzied me. I sank onto the bed, running my hands over the soft bedding.

"I'll leave you to settle in," Kye said. "If you need anything --"

"Wait," I blurted. He paused, eyebrows raised. "I… Thank you."

A small smile touched his lips. "Rest well, Yulia." The door clicked shut behind him.

Alone, I curled into myself. Tears threatened, but I blinked them back. This room, this bed -- my mind struggled to accept it as real. As mine. I'd dreamed of escape for so long. Now that it was here, I felt… lost. Unmoored.

But safe. For the first time in years, truly safe.

A soft knock startled me from my thoughts. I tensed, eyeing the door warily.

"Hello?" a young voice called, barely audible. "I'm Clover. Kye asked me to bring you some clothes."

I hesitated, then crossed to the door, cracking it open. A petite girl stood there, probably no more than five or six, arms full of folded fabric. Her eyes, warm brown and wise beyond her years, met mine.

"You can leave them," I murmured.

Clover nodded, setting the pile just inside. "I was told to let you know I'm down the hall if you need anything. They thought you might be more comfortable with me than the men."

As she turned to go, I noticed scars tracing her arms that matched the ones on her face. My breath caught. She paused, glancing back.

"Thank you," I managed.

A small smile touched her lips before she disappeared.

I shut the door, leaning against it. My mind raced. Another girl, rescued? What was this place?

Heavy footsteps approached. Kye's voice rumbled through the wood. "Everything all right, Yulia?"

I swallowed hard. "Yes. I… the clothes. Thank you."

"Good." His tone softened. "Remember, you're safe here. No one will hurt you again. I promise."

I sank to the floor. Tears burned, but didn't fall.

The silence engulfed me as Kye's footsteps faded away. I pushed myself up from the floor, my legs trembling slightly. The room seemed to close in, unfamiliar and daunting. I wrapped my arms around myself, seeking comfort in the gesture.

My gaze drifted to the pile of clothes Clover had left. Clean. New. A stark contrast to the tattered remnants of my old life that still clung to me. I ran my fingers over the soft fabric, marveling at the simple kindness.

The bed called to me, its promise of rest both alluring and terrifying. What dreams -- what nightmares -- awaited me there? I perched on the edge, my body heavy with exhaustion.

"Breathe, Yulia," I whispered to myself, my voice barely audible. "Just breathe."

I closed my eyes, willing my racing thoughts to slow. The day's events swirled in my mind -- the cold metal of the knife, the roar of the motorcycle, Kye's steady gaze. It felt surreal, like a fever dream I couldn't shake.

My hand unconsciously traced the faint scars on my arm. The past whispered, threatening to drag me back. But here, in this strange room, surrounded by people I didn't know… was it possible to outrun the past?

I lay back, sinking into the mattress. The ceiling

blurred as exhaustion tugged at me. "Safe," I murmured, testing the word on my tongue. It felt foreign, fragile. As sleep began to claim me, I clung to Kye's promise like a lifeline. No matter what tomorrow brought, for tonight at least, I was protected. The thought followed me into an uneasy slumber, where motorcycles roared and scarred arms reached out to catch me as I fell.

Chapter One

Yulia
Eleven Years Later

I paused in the doorway to the kitchen, my breath catching at the sight before me. Salvation stood at the stove, his broad back to me as he stirred something that filled the air with a rich, savory scent. Beside him, Clover frowned at a textbook, pencil tapping against the page. Salvation turned to point at something, his voice a low, patient rumble. The domesticity of it struck me like a physical blow -- this simple moment between father and daughter. A life I'd never known, never thought I'd be part of. Yet here I was, hovering at the edge, not quite in, not quite out. Always watching.

"If you divide both sides by three, what do you get?" Salvation asked, not missing a beat as he expertly chopped some herbs, the knife flashing in his steady hands.

Clover sighed dramatically. "X equals twelve."

"Good." He scraped the herbs into the stew. "Now try the next one."

I leaned against the doorframe, mesmerized by his movements. For such a powerful man, Salvation handled each task with surprising gentleness. Not just the cooking, but also the way he handled Clover. My own father had been nothing like Salvation. I couldn't help but be mesmerized by the man's every move. His forearms flexed with each motion, the sleeves of his T-shirt stretched tight around solid biceps.

"This one has two variables," Clover complained, yanking me from my thoughts.

"Start with what you know," Salvation replied, giving the stew a good stir. "Isolate one variable, then solve for it."

The scent of our dinner cooking made my stomach growl. I hadn't realized how hungry I was until now. Salvation glanced over his shoulder at the sound, and our eyes met briefly. My cheeks warmed. I looked away first.

"Dinner's almost ready," he said, his voice softer than when he'd been explaining equations. "Twenty minutes, maybe."

I nodded, not trusting my voice. When I looked up again, he'd already turned back to the stove. My gaze traced the strong line of his shoulders, the way his dark hair curled slightly at the nape of his neck. In moments like this, I could almost forget he was Kye, the man who'd rescued me. The man I'd married -- on paper, at least -- for protection. Here, in this kitchen, he was just Salvation. A man cooking dinner for his family.

Family. The word still felt foreign, uncomfortable. Like clothes that didn't quite fit. I shifted my weight, and my sleeve rode up. The silvery scars on my wrist caught the light. A harsh reminder of where I'd been, what I'd almost done. Well, what I'd nearly done *again* because that hadn't been my first attempt. I tugged my sleeve down quickly, heart pounding.

"You just going to stand there all night?" Clover asked, breaking into my thoughts. Her eyes, too knowing for her sixteen years, flickered between me and Salvation.

"I... no." I pushed away from the doorframe and approached the table, sliding into the chair across from her. "How's the homework going?"

"It's going," she muttered, then brightened. "But

Dad's a good teacher."

Salvation snorted softly at the stove. "Don't let your actual teachers hear that."

I watched as he stirred the pot, then bent to check something in the oven. The simple domesticity of it all made my chest ache with longing. For what, I wasn't entirely sure.

"The trick with these equations," Salvation continued, straightening up and wiping his hands on a towel tucked into his back pocket, "is not to overcomplicate them. Break them down, one step at a time."

If only life were that simple, I thought. *Break down the complications. Solve for the unknown.*

Salvation moved to the refrigerator, pulling out a bottle of water. His T-shirt rode up slightly, revealing a strip of tanned skin above his jeans. I swallowed hard and forced my gaze back to the table.

"Dad, can you check this one?" Clover pushed her notebook across the table.

Salvation set his water down and leaned over her shoulder, one hand braced on the table. His proximity made my skin prickle with awareness. He smelled like spices and something uniquely him -- clean sweat and soap.

"You dropped a negative here," he said, pointing. "Try again."

Clover groaned but bent back over her work. Salvation returned to the stove, stirring the contents of the pot before adding another handful of chopped herbs.

I realized I'd been staring again when Clover's foot nudged mine under the table. I blinked, meeting her gaze. Her eyes darted meaningfully between me and Salvation, one eyebrow raised in a question I didn't want to answer. Heat crept up my neck. I shook my head slightly, a silent plea for her to drop it.

Instead, she leaned forward, her voice dropping to a whisper. "If you don't make a move, nothing will ever change."

My mouth fell open. I snapped it shut, mortified. "I don't --" I started, but the words died in my throat as Salvation glanced over, his expression curious.

"Everything okay?" he asked.

"Fine," I managed, my voice unnaturally high. "Just… math. Complicated."

He nodded slowly, his eyes lingering on my flushed face before turning back to his cooking.

Clover smirked. I kicked her gently under the table but couldn't quite summon any real annoyance. Instead, a bubble of nervous laughter threatened to escape me. This girl, with her too-wise eyes and matter-of-fact statements, had somehow become important to me in the years since I'd arrived. "It's true," she mouthed silently, nodding toward Salvation's back.

I ducked my head, letting my hair fall forward to hide my burning cheeks. Maybe it was true. Maybe I *did* need to make a move. But the thought alone was terrifying -- more frightening, somehow, than the blade I'd once held to my wrist.

Because this time, I had something to lose.

Clover closed her textbook with a decisive snap, shooting me one last knowing look before gathering her papers. "I should put these away. And finish that reading for English. I'll come fix my plate when I'm finished, so don't wait for me."

I recognized the excuse for what it was -- a deliberate exit, leaving Salvation and me alone. My heart jumped into my throat. I wasn't ready for this.

Not yet. Not with her words still humming in my ears.

"Don't forget we need to leave early tomorrow," Salvation reminded her, not looking up from the pot he was stirring. "Doctor's appointment before school."

Clover rolled her eyes. "Like I could forget. You've reminded me three times today."

"Make it four," he replied, a smile in his voice.

She huffed dramatically but grinned as she tucked her books under her arm. "Night, Dad." She paused at the doorway, looking back at me. "Night, Yulia."

"Goodnight," I managed. Her footsteps faded down the hallway, each one taking my courage with it. The kitchen suddenly felt smaller, the air thicker.

I sat frozen at the table, hyperaware of every sound -- the bubbling of the pot and even Salvation's steady breathing. He moved around the kitchen with practiced ease, seemingly oblivious to my presence. Or perhaps just accustomed to it. After all, this was our routine most nights. He cooked. I watched. We ate. We existed in the same space without really occupying it together.

My fingers picked at a loose thread on my sleeve. We'd been married for about eleven years now -- on paper only, as he'd promised that first night. A marriage of protection, nothing more. He'd given me safety, stability. A home. But in moments like this, with just the two of us, I couldn't help but wonder if there could be more.

Salvation opened the oven, releasing a cloud of fragrant steam. The muscles in his back flexed as he bent to check whatever was roasting inside. My mouth went dry.

"Looks good," he murmured, more to himself than to me.

I swallowed hard. *Yeah, you do.* "What are you making?"

He glanced over his shoulder, surprise flickering across his face at the sound of my voice. "Beef stew. And bread." He gestured to the oven. "Nothing fancy."

But it was fancy to me. I'd been stuck with institutional food at various boarding schools for about a decade, then it had been months of barely eating at all as I adjusted to the path my life had taken. Not to mention, my family had hired cooks. My mother wouldn't have been caught dead in the kitchen except to bark orders at people. She might have been sweet to her daughters, but she tended to take out her frustration on the servants. These home-cooked meals had been a luxury.

You'd think after all this time I'd be used to it, but some part of me still worried it would all be yanked out of my hands at a moment's notice.

Salvation returned to the stove, lifting the lid from the pot to stir the contents. The rhythmic motion of his arm, the concentration on his face as he tasted from the wooden spoon -- these small details fascinated me. Made my heart race in a way that had nothing to do with fear.

Before I could second-guess myself, I pushed away from the table and approached the counter. I picked up a dish towel, folding and unfolding it between my fingers. "Can I help with anything?" I asked, my voice softer than I'd intended.

Salvation glanced up, his calm gaze meeting mine briefly before returning to the cutting board. "Just rest. I've got this," he replied.

My shoulders dropped slightly. My fingers tightened on the towel. Of course. I should have expected that response. It was the same one he always gave me. "Right," I said, hating the hint of disappointment that crept into my voice. I returned to the table, watching him work. The silence between us grew heavier, filled with all the things I couldn't say. All the things he wouldn't say.

Salvation moved to the sink, washing his hands before drying them on another towel. His wedding ring -- the simple gold band we'd bought outside the courthouse -- caught the light. A reminder of promises made, boundaries established. Although, at the time, I hadn't realized our wedding had been faked. A hacker had taken care of everything, and the ceremony had been for show, mostly for me. It was one of the many kindnesses Salvation had given me in our years together.

"Should be ready in about ten minutes," he said, breaking the silence.

I nodded, though he wasn't looking at me. "It smells wonderful."

A small smile touched his lips. "Clover's favorite."

Always about Clover. Never about us. I couldn't blame him -- she was his daughter in all the ways that mattered. I was just... what? A responsibility? A charity case? A stranger he'd married to keep safe?

The thought stung, though I knew it wasn't fair. Salvation had never pretended our arrangement was anything other than what it was. A marriage on paper. He'd never promised love, never suggested our relationship would evolve into something more intimate.

And yet... the way he sometimes looked at me when he thought I wouldn't notice. The gentle care he took to never push me, never rush me. The way he'd touch my shoulder, just briefly, when passing by -- so careful, so restrained. All those things always gave me hope we could have something more.

I watched as he set plates on the counter, his movements efficient, practiced. There was something mesmerizing about his hands -- strong, capable, but never threatening. Never cruel.

So different from the hands that had hurt me before.

"Yulia?" His voice pulled me from my thoughts. "Everything okay?"

I blinked, realizing I'd been staring. Again. "Yes. Sorry. Just… thinking."

He studied me for a moment, his expression unreadable. Then he nodded and turned back to his task. The clock on the wall ticked loudly in the silence. Outside, the sun had set, turning the kitchen window into a mirror that reflected our odd little tableau. Salvation at the stove, me at the table. Close enough to touch, separated by an invisible wall neither of us seemed able to breach.

If you don't make a move, nothing will ever change. Clover's words echoed in my mind. But what move could I make? How did one bridge such a gap? Especially when I wasn't even sure what waited on the other side.

Salvation reached for the oven mitts, his shirt riding up again to reveal that same strip of skin. My pulse quickened. This attraction, this longing -- it had been growing for years. At first, I'd dismissed it as gratitude, as the natural response to being rescued. But it had deepened, evolved into something more complex. More terrifying.

I looked down at my hands, at the faint scars on my wrists. Reminders of a different life, a different Yulia. The girl who had given up. Who had seen no future worth living for. That girl would never have imagined sitting in this warm kitchen, watching this man, feeling this ache of wanting something more.

Maybe that was progress. Maybe that was enough. There was a chance it would have to be, that Salvation would never want anything more from me.

My heart pounded against my ribs like a trapped bird. The words I needed to say had been building inside me for so very long. Simple words. Honest words. *I want more. I feel something for you. This marriage doesn't have to be just on paper.*

My fingers twisted in my lap as I watched Salvation's back, the steady movement of his shoulders as he worked. *Just say it. The worst he can do is say no.* But that wasn't true. The worst he could do was look at me with pity. With regret. With the gentle rejection I'd seen him use on the club women who sometimes flirted with him.

I drew a deep breath, trying to calm the tremor in my hands. We couldn't continue like this forever -- orbiting each other, never touching, never acknowledging the current that sometimes sparked between us when our gazes met. When our fingers accidentally brushed passing the salt. When he stood too close behind me, reaching for something on a high shelf.

Salvation turned to check the bread in the oven again. *Now. Say it now.*

My throat tightened. My pulse hammered in my ears, nearly drowning out the soft sounds of cooking. I licked my dry lips.

"Still need to set the table," he said, not turning around.

"I'll do it," I said, grateful for the momentary reprieve. I stood, legs unsteady, and moved to the counter where he'd placed the plates earlier. The familiar task gave my hands something to do, my mind something to focus on besides the words lodged in my throat.

Plates. Silverware. Napkins. Simple tasks. Safe actions. But as I finished, the moment of truth loomed again. Salvation turned off the burner, shifting the pot to a cool element. Dinner was almost ready. She'd said she wouldn't, but it wouldn't be the first time she changed her mind. If I was going to speak, it had to be now, just in case Clover returned. Before we settled into our usual routine of polite conversation about safe topics.

I inhaled sharply, hands gripping the back of a chair for support. "Salvation, I --" I began, but stopped abruptly. The words died on my lips as he turned to face me, wooden spoon still in hand, his expression open and attentive.

His eyes -- those gentle, steady eyes -- fixed on mine. Waiting. The moment stretched between us, pregnant with possibility. My heart thundered so loudly I was certain he must hear it. *Say it! Tell him.* But my courage faltered, dissolving like sugar in hot tea.

"Never mind," I finally said. "It's nothing."

Salvation studied my face, his gaze lingering longer than usual. Something flickered in his eyes -- curiosity? Concern? Something else entirely? For a breathless moment, I thought he might press me, might ask what I'd been about to say.

Instead, he nodded slowly and turned back to the stove.

But something had shifted. I felt it in the air between us, a subtle change in pressure. The way his shoulders tensed slightly. The careful way he avoided looking at me again as he took down two bowls and served the stew, then put slices of bread onto the small plates.

I moved mechanically, placing glasses on the table, filling them with water. We danced around each other in the small kitchen, suddenly hyperaware of the other's presence. When his arm brushed mine as he set the rest of the bread on the table, I flinched as if burned. He murmured an apology, stepping back quickly.

"Should I call Clover?" I asked, desperate to break the awkward silence.

"You heard her. She'll eat when she's ready," he replied, his voice carefully neutral.

I nodded, taking my usual seat at the table. Salvation remained standing, busying himself at the counter longer than necessary. The tension between us stretched taut, a rubber band pulled to its limit.

What would have happened if I'd spoken? If I'd laid my feelings bare? Would he have rejected me gently? Or worse, would he have accepted out of obligation, out of pity for the broken girl he'd rescued?

Or -- and this possibility terrified me most -- would he have revealed that he felt the same?

Salvation finally sat across from me, the wooden chair creaking under his weight. His eyes met mine briefly before dropping to his bowl.

"Smells delicious," I offered, my voice unnaturally bright.

He nodded, breaking off a piece of bread. "Thanks."

Another silence fell, heavy with unspoken words. I pushed my stew around with my spoon, appetite gone. The moment had passed. My chance slipped away like water through cupped hands.

Clover's footsteps sounded in the hallway,

drawing closer. Soon she would join us, and the strange tension would be diluted by her presence. Everything would return to normal -- or what passed for normal in our unusual arrangement.

But as Salvation's gaze briefly met mine again across the table, I knew something fundamental had changed. That almost-conversation, those unspoken words, hung between us now. A question mark. A possibility.

If you don't make a move, nothing will ever change.

I hadn't made my move. Not really. But something had changed anyway. And I wasn't sure if it was terrifying or exhilarating.

Chapter Two

Yulia

The spring sun beat down on my shoulders as I cut across the compound, my steps quick and purposeful despite the uncertainty churning in my stomach. Eleven years at the Reckless Kings had taught me the quickest routes between buildings, how to avoid the areas where Prospects congregated, and most importantly -- who to trust with secrets that burned in my chest like embers. Today, that knowledge led me straight to the picnic area behind the main clubhouse, where I knew Whisper would be enjoying her midday break.

My hands trembled slightly, and I shoved them into my pockets. I'd rehearsed this conversation a dozen times since last night, when Salvation's gaze had lingered on mine across the dinner table, making my heart race and my courage falter. But practice did nothing to ease the knot in my throat now.

I spotted her beneath the shade of an old oak tree, perched on a picnic table with a book in her lap. Whisper -- Brick's adopted daughter and Forge's wife -- was the club's unofficial voice of reason. You would think it would have been Lyssa, the President's woman, but she tended to be more aggressive than Whisper. If anyone could help me make sense of the mess inside my head, it would be her.

She looked up as I approached, a smile warming her face. "Yulia. This is a surprise." She closed her book, marking her place with a finger. "Everything okay?"

"I…" The words stuck in my throat. I took a deep

breath and sat beside her on the bench, leaving enough distance between us to feel comfortable. My fingers found the hem of my shirt, worrying the fabric between them. "I need advice."

Whisper nodded, waiting patiently. The gentle breeze lifted strands of her hair, carrying the scent of her light perfume. In the distance, motorcycles revved as members came and went, but our corner remained peaceful.

"It's about Salvation," I finally said, my accent thickening as it always did when I was nervous. "About… us."

"I figured it might be." Her voice held no judgment, just quiet understanding.

I glanced at her, surprised. "Was I that obvious?"

She smiled. "Only to someone who's been watching. The way you look at him when you think no one notices. The way he makes excuses to be near you at club gatherings." She shrugged. "What's on your mind?"

The dam broke. Words poured out of me in a rush. "I don't know what to do. We've been married for eleven years, but it's never been… real. At first, it was just about protection. I was sixteen, terrified. He saved my life. The marriage was just papers, a shield against my father's enemies. Empty words and nothing more."

Whisper nodded, her eyes soft with understanding.

"Then we became… friends, I guess. Roommates. He raised Clover. I finished school. We built a life together, but always with this… distance." I swallowed hard. "Separate rooms. Separate lives under one roof."

"And now?" Whisper prompted gently.

"Now I can't stop thinking about him." The

admission burned my cheeks. "The way he moves. His voice. His hands." I shook my head, frustration building. "Last night, I almost told him. The words were right there, but I couldn't say them."

"Why not?"

I bit my lip, staring down at my fidgeting hands. "What if I tell him how I feel and he doesn't want me that way? We're technically married, but at the same time, we aren't, if that makes sense. If he asks me to leave, I'll have nowhere to go."

The fear I'd been carrying for so long finally had voice, and it sounded pathetic even to my own ears. But Whisper didn't laugh. Instead, she reached out slowly -- giving me time to pull away -- and placed her hand over mine, stilling my restless fingers.

"Yulia, look at me." When I met her gaze, her eyes were firm but kind. "That man has protected you for eleven years. He's not going to suddenly change because you admit you have feelings for him."

"You don't know that," I whispered.

"I do." Her confidence was unwavering. "I've known Kye a bit longer than you. He doesn't make commitments lightly. When he pledged to protect you, he meant it -- for life. Not just from external threats, but from pain. From fear." She squeezed my hand gently. "He would cut off his own arm before he'd hurt you."

Her words warmed something inside me but doubt still gnawed. "Then why the distance? All these years, he's never… indicated he wanted more."

Whisper's expression softened. "Have you considered that maybe he's afraid of the same thing? That if he crossed that line, you'd feel trapped? Obligated?" She released my hand and leaned back. "The man rescued you from the edge of death, Yulia.

He's painfully aware of how vulnerable you were. How much power he had over your situation."

I hadn't thought of it that way. The idea that Salvation -- strong, confident Salvation -- might be as uncertain as I was seemed impossible. Yet…

"But what if I'm misreading everything?" I looked away when Whisper's gaze became too knowing. "What if he only sees me as… a responsibility? A friend at most?"

"There's only one way to find out." Her voice was gentle but firm. "Be honest with him."

The thought made my stomach clench with terror. I wrapped my arms around myself, suddenly cold despite the warm day. "I don't know if I can."

"You survived your father's enemies. You survived your own darkest moment." Whisper's voice dropped lower. "You're stronger than you think, Yulia."

Maybe she was right. Maybe I was. But as I sat there, the spring breeze carrying the sounds of the compound around us, I couldn't help but think of all I stood to lose. The home I'd built. The fragile peace I'd found. And most of all, the man who'd been my constant for eleven years -- first as savior, then as friend, and now as… something I couldn't quite name.

"What if I tell him," I whispered, "and everything changes?"

Whisper smiled, a knowing light in her eyes. "That's the point, isn't it? Change is scary. But some things are worth the risk." She glanced toward the clubhouse, where several members were emerging. "Take it from someone who knows -- loving a Reckless King isn't simple. But if it's the right one, it's worth every moment of fear."

I followed her gaze, my heart thudding painfully

in my chest. Somewhere in that compound, Salvation was going about his day, completely unaware of the storm inside me. Unaware that tonight, perhaps, everything between us might change.

For better or worse.

* * *

Salvation

I found Beast alone in the clubhouse office, hunched over paperwork with a scowl that would've sent Prospects running. But I'd known the man too long to be intimidated. Hell, I'd patched in under his leadership, watched him build the Reckless Kings into what we were today. If anyone could make sense of the mess in my head, it was him. I knocked once on the doorframe, my knuckles rapping against the wood sharper than intended.

Beast looked up, his expression shifting from irritation to curiosity. "Salvation. What's up?"

"Got a minute?" I asked, my voice rougher than normal.

He gestured to the chair across from his desk, closing the ledger he'd been reviewing. "Something wrong?"

I shut the door behind me, needing the privacy. The usual clubhouse sounds -- pool balls cracking, music thumping, brothers laughing -- became muffled. I sank into the chair but couldn't get comfortable, my body tense with unspoken words.

"Not wrong, exactly." I ran a hand through my hair, suddenly feeling like a Prospect again instead of a patched member of eleven years. "I need… advice."

Beast leaned back in his chair, arms crossed over his chest. His eyes narrowed slightly, reading me with the same precision he used to evaluate threats to the club. "What kind of advice?"

"Personal." The word felt inadequate. I stood again, restless energy driving me to pace the small office. "It's about Yulia."

Understanding dawned in Beast's eyes. He nodded slowly. "Been wondering when we'd have this conversation."

That stopped me mid-stride. "What?"

Beast huffed out something close to a laugh. "Brother, you've been married to that woman for what, eleven years now? On paper only, yeah, but still. You share a home. You've watched her grow from a scared kid into a woman." He shrugged. "Things change."

I pressed my palms against the edge of his desk, leaning forward. "That's just it. I've noticed things changing between us. The way she looks at me sometimes..." I trailed off, unsure how to explain the electricity sometimes sparking between us in quiet moments. The way her gaze lingered on mine across rooms. How my body had become hyperaware of hers -- her scent, her proximity, the accidental brushes of skin against skin.

"And?" Beast prompted.

"And I don't know what to do about it." I pushed away from the desk, resuming my pacing. "If I make a move, I might scare her. After everything she's been through, I don't want to cause her any harm."

Beast watched me, his expression unreadable. "What exactly did she go through? You never told the club the details. Don't get me wrong, we heard some before we decided to rescue her, but I have a feeling our intel wasn't all of it."

I shook my head. "Not my story to tell. But it was bad. She was sixteen, Beast. Suicidal. Her father's enemies were after her. The teacher at her boarding school…" My hands clenched into fists at the memory of the bruises, the cuts on her wrists, the hollow emptiness in her eyes when Hawk first brought her to us.

"And you married her to protect her," Beast finished. "Made her legal family so her father's people couldn't touch her."

"Yeah." I stopped by the window, staring out at the compound without really seeing it. "It was never supposed to be a real marriage. Just papers. Protection."

"But now?"

I turned to face him. "Now I can't stop thinking about her. As a woman, not just someone I need to protect." The admission felt like weights lifted from my shoulders. "And I think… maybe she feels the same. But what if I'm wrong? What if I'm just seeing what I want to see?"

Beast leaned forward, resting his forearms on the desk. "You afraid of ruining what you have? The friendship?"

"That's part of it." I sank back into the chair, suddenly exhausted. "But it's more than that. What if I push for more and it triggers something? Makes her remember…" I couldn't finish the thought.

"You think she still sees you as just protection? A safe harbor?"

I shrugged helplessly. "I don't know. Maybe. And then there's Clover to consider."

Beast raised an eyebrow. "What about her?"

"She's sixteen now. Same age Yulia was when I married her." I leaned forward, elbows on my knees. "She and Yulia are close. What happens if Clover thinks I'm taking advantage? Or if things between Yulia and me go bad? It would tear Clover apart."

A small smile played at the corner of Beast's mouth. "You always did overthink shit."

"This isn't funny," I said, my words holding more bite than usual.

"Never said it was." Beast stood, moving to the small bar in the corner of the office. He poured two fingers of whiskey into each of two glasses and handed one to me. "But you're spinning scenarios that haven't happened yet. Making decisions based on fear."

I accepted the glass but didn't drink. "It's not fear. It's caution."

"Call it what you want." Beast leaned against his desk, looking down at me. "That girl's been living with you for eleven years. She's not the same scared teenager you rescued. She's a woman now. Twenty-seven, right?"

I nodded.

"And in all those years, she's chosen to stay. With you." Beast took a sip of his whiskey. "That tells me something."

I rolled the glass between my palms, watching the amber liquid catch the light. "What about Clover?"

"Your daughter's not stupid. She sees more than you think." Beast's voice softened slightly. "Kids adapt. Especially kids like Clover who've already weathered hard times."

"And if Yulia doesn't feel the same?" The question that had been haunting me for what felt like forever finally had a voice.

Beast shrugged. "Then you respect that and move on. But at least you'll know." He fixed me with his steady gaze. "The question you need to ask yourself is whether what you might gain is worth the risk."

I downed the whiskey in one burning swallow,

welcoming the heat that spread through my chest. "And if she pulls away? Leaves?"

"That's her choice. While marriage is a forever thing around here, your case is different. If Yulia wants to move on, then we'll let her." Beast's words were firm but not unkind. "You can't protect someone from their own decisions, Salvation. Not even someone you love."

Love. The word hit me like a physical blow. Was that what this was? This constant awareness, this need to ensure her happiness, this ache to be closer to her?

"How did you know?" I asked quietly. "With Lyssa?"

A rare smile crossed Beast's face at the mention of his wife. "I didn't. Not for sure. I just knew I couldn't imagine my life without her in it." He set his empty glass on the desk. "Sometimes you just have to take the leap, brother. Despite the risk. Despite the fear."

I stood, setting my glass beside his. "Thanks for the advice."

Beast clapped me on the shoulder. "Don't overthink it. That woman's been waiting for you to see her -- really see her -- for a long time now."

His words followed me as I left the office, threading through the crowded main room of the clubhouse. Had Yulia really been waiting? Had I been blind to what was right in front of me all these years?

Only one way to find out. But the thought of crossing that line, of potentially disrupting the careful balance we'd established, still made my heart race with something between anticipation and dread.

Tonight. I'll talk to her tonight.

* * *

Yulia

I lingered in the kitchen doorway, my heart lodged somewhere in my throat as I watched Salvation pull ingredients from the refrigerator. Since my conversation with Whisper that afternoon, every nerve ending in my body seemed heightened, attuned to his presence in a way that made my skin prickle with awareness. The kitchen suddenly felt too small, too intimate -- a space where we'd coexisted for years without acknowledging the current that sometimes sparked between us. Tonight, that current felt like a live wire, dangerous and irresistible.

"You just going to stand there?" Salvation asked without turning around, his voice deeper than usual.

I stepped into the kitchen, forcing my feet to move naturally. "What are you making?"

"Chicken stir-fry." He set a package of chicken breasts on the cutting board. "Figured it was quick. Been a long day."

I nodded, though he wasn't looking at me. The kitchen enveloped us in its familiar comfort -- the soft hum of the refrigerator, the warm yellow light above the stove, the lingering scent of this morning's coffee. Through the open window, cool evening air carried the distant sound of motorcycles and the sweet scent of spring flowers. It should have felt normal. Routine. But nothing about tonight felt routine.

"I can help," I said, moving to the sink to wash my hands. "What do you need?"

Salvation glanced at me, surprise flickering across his face. "You don't have to --"

"I want to." I dried my hands on a dish towel, summoning a confidence I didn't entirely feel. "Just tell me what to do."

He studied me for a moment, then nodded

toward the vegetables on the counter. "You could chop those. Bell peppers, onion, broccoli."

I took a knife from the block and set to work beside him, acutely conscious of how our arms nearly touched as we stood at the counter. The knife felt awkward in my hand -- I hadn't done much cooking over the years, content to let Salvation handle that domain. But lately, I'd been trying more, finding excuses to spend time with him in these domestic moments.

"Like this?" I asked, showing him my attempt at dicing the bell pepper.

He glanced over, his gaze lingering on my hands. "Smaller pieces, if you can." His fingers brushed mine as he repositioned the knife in my grip. "Like this."

That brief touch sent electricity racing up my arm. I swallowed hard, forcing myself to focus on the vegetable and not on the heat of his body so close to mine.

Whisper's words echoed in my head: *Be honest with him.* But how could I form words when my pulse hammered at the base of my throat, when every fiber of my being seemed drawn to him like a magnet?

We worked in silence for several minutes, the only sounds the rhythmic chopping of knives and the sizzle of oil heating in the pan. I snuck glances at him when I thought he wouldn't notice -- the concentration in his brow as he sliced the chicken into perfect strips, the play of muscles in his forearms, the way his dark hair curled slightly at his collar.

When our hips bumped as we both reached for the cutting board, I nearly jumped.

"Sorry," we said in unison, then shared an awkward smile.

"Cramped space," Salvation murmured,

stepping back to give me room.

But I didn't want room. I wanted closer. The realization shocked me with its intensity.

"It's fine," I said, my voice sounding strange to my own ears. "I don't mind."

His gaze met mine, something dark and questioning in their depths. Had he spoken with someone too? Something felt different about him tonight -- a tension in his shoulders, a deliberateness to his movements that hadn't been there before.

We continued preparing the meal, orbiting each other in the small kitchen like planets caught in each other's gravity. When he reached past me for the salt, his chest brushed against my shoulder. When I moved to the sink, he shifted to let me pass, his hand briefly settling on my waist to steady me. Each touch, however fleeting, left my skin burning.

The stir-fry sizzled in the pan, filling the kitchen with the aroma of garlic and ginger. Salvation stirred it with practiced ease, adding soy sauce and a splash of something from a bottle I didn't recognize.

"We need the red pepper flakes," he said, glancing at the spice rack mounted on the wall above the stove. "For heat."

I followed his gaze to the small jar on the highest shelf -- just out of my reach. "I'll get it."

I stretched up on my tiptoes, fingers grasping for the jar. It remained stubbornly beyond my reach.

Suddenly, Salvation was behind me, his chest pressed against my back as he reached up. "Here," he murmured, his breath warm against my ear. "Let me."

Time seemed to stop. His body caged mine against the counter, solid and warm. I could feel the steady thud of his heart against my back, smell the familiar scent of his soap mixed with leather and something uniquely him. My breath caught in my throat.

He grabbed the jar but didn't move away. Instead, he lowered his arm slowly, his body still pressed against mine. I turned within the circle of his arms, my back now against the counter, my face tilted up to his.

Our eyes locked. The spice jar dangled forgotten from his fingers.

"Yulia," he said, my name a rough whisper.

I couldn't speak, couldn't breathe. All I could do was look up at him, at the question in his eyes, at the way his gaze dropped to my lips. Slowly, deliberately, he leaned in. My eyes fluttered closed, my heart hammering so loudly I was sure he could hear it.

I felt the heat of his breath against my lips, the slightest brush of contact --

"Is dinner ready yet? I'm starving!"

Clover's voice shattered the moment like glass. We sprang apart, Salvation nearly dropping the spice jar as he stepped back. I turned to the stove, my cheeks burning, hands shaking as I pretended to check the food.

"Five more minutes," Salvation answered, his voice unnaturally gruff. "Just finishing up."

I risked a glance at him. His jaw was tight, frustration evident in the set of his shoulders as he added the red pepper flakes to the pan. When our eyes met briefly, I saw something smoldering there that made my stomach flip.

Clover leaned against the doorframe, looking between us with narrowed eyes. "Did I interrupt something?"

"No," we said in unison, too quickly.

Her lips curved into a knowing smile. "Right.

Sure, I didn't." She pushed away from the doorframe. "I'll set the table, then."

As she gathered plates from the cabinet, I continued stirring the stir-fry, trying to calm my racing heart. So close. We'd been so close. And from the heated look Salvation had given me, the moment hadn't been one-sided.

"Almost done?" he asked quietly, coming to stand beside me again.

I nodded, not trusting my voice.

His fingers brushed mine on the handle of the wooden spoon, a touch so brief it could have been accidental. But when I looked up, the intensity in his eyes told me nothing about it had been accidental at all.

"Later," he murmured, his voice low enough that only I could hear. "We need to talk."

It wasn't a question, but I nodded anyway, a mix of anticipation and terror swirling in my chest. Later. When we were alone again. When there would be no interruptions.

The thought made me tremble.

Chapter Three

Salvation

I gripped the steering wheel tighter as we approached the county fairgrounds, the words I hadn't said to Yulia still burning in my throat days after our moment in the kitchen. We hadn't found time to be alone since Clover interrupted us -- or maybe we were both avoiding it. Either way, the tension between us had only grown, crackling like electricity whenever our gazes met across rooms. Now, confined in the cab of my truck with Yulia beside me and Clover chattering excitedly from the back seat, I felt like a live wire about to spark.

"Dad, you passed it!" Clover leaned forward, jabbing her finger toward a dirt lot already filling with cars. "The entrance is right there."

I grunted, checking my mirrors before making a sharp turn. "Saw it."

Yulia's hand braced against the dashboard at the sudden movement. Her sleeve rode up, revealing the faint silver scars on her wrist -- a reminder of how we'd met, of how far she'd come. She caught me looking and tugged her sleeve down, a flush creeping up her neck.

"Sorry," I muttered, swinging into the makeshift parking lot. "Wasn't paying attention."

"It's okay," she said softly. Her accent, which always seemed stronger when her emotions ran high, still got to me even after eleven years.

I found a spot near the back of the lot and killed the engine. Families streamed past us toward the fairground entrance, children tugging at parents' hands, teenagers laughing in clusters. Normal people living normal lives. Sometimes I forgot what that looked like.

"Can we go now?" Clover was already halfway out the door, practically vibrating with impatience.

"Hold up," I said, pocketing my keys. "We stick together. Fair's gonna be packed."

Clover rolled her eyes but waited, bouncing on her toes as Yulia and I exited the truck. I locked it, then hesitated, unsure where to position myself as we walked. Yulia solved the problem, falling into step on my left while Clover took my right. The space between Yulia and me felt charged, too wide and too narrow all at once.

The fairgrounds burst with noise and color, an assault on the senses after the relative quiet of the compound. Carnival rides whirled against the clear sky. Game booths lined the paths, barkers calling out to passersby, stuffed animals dangling from overhead hooks. The scent of frying dough, sugar, and grilled meat hung thick in the air.

"Look!" Clover pointed toward a towering roller coaster, its track twisting like a metal serpent. "Can we ride that one first?"

My stomach knotted at the thought. "How about we start with something that won't make me puke?"

Yulia laughed, the sound unexpectedly bright. She quickly covered her mouth, but her eyes crinkled at the corners. Something warm unfurled in my chest.

"Sorry," she said, tucking a strand of dark honey hair behind her ear. The simple gesture drew my attention to the delicate curve of her jaw, the soft skin of her neck. "I just pictured you, big scary biker, afraid of a carnival ride."

"Not afraid," I corrected, the corner of my mouth

twitching. "Just practical."

Clover groaned. "You're both so boring. Fine, let's do the Ferris wheel first. Even old people like that one."

"Old?" I reached for her, but she danced away, laughing.

"You heard me, Dad."

I shook my head, unable to suppress my smile. My daughter -- because that's what she was, biology be damned -- had Carina's sass and my stubbornness. A dangerous combination.

We approached the ticket booth, and I pulled out my wallet. "How many?"

"Fifty," Clover said immediately.

I raised an eyebrow. "Twenty each. That's plenty."

I paid for the tickets, painfully aware of Yulia standing close beside me, her arm occasionally brushing against mine. When the ticket seller handed me the strips, our fingers touched briefly as I passed some to Yulia. The contact sent a jolt up my arm, and our eyes met for a charged moment before she looked away, cheeks flushed.

"Ferris wheel's this way," Clover announced, already moving ahead.

I placed my hand lightly on Yulia's lower back to guide her through the crowd, a touch that would have been casual years ago but now felt fraught with meaning. She stiffened briefly, then relaxed into it, letting me steer her along the packed midway.

The Ferris wheel loomed ahead, its spokes turning lazily against the sky. The line moved quickly, and soon we were handing over our tickets to a weathered man with sun-leathered skin.

"Two per car," he said, barely looking up.

Clover immediately hopped into an empty car. "I'll ride alone."

Before I could protest, she grinned and added, "You two can share. I won't mind."

The operator shrugged and locked her in, then gestured to the next car. I met Yulia's gaze, finding a question there -- and something else, something that made my pulse quicken.

"After you," I said, my voice rougher than intended.

She slid into the small compartment, and I followed, acutely aware of how the space forced us close together, thighs touching, shoulders brushing. The operator closed the safety bar, locking us in place.

"Enjoy the ride," he said, then added with a wink, "Beautiful family you got there."

Heat crawled up my neck. "Thanks," I managed, not correcting him. Beside me, Yulia ducked her head, but not before I caught the smile playing at the corners of her mouth.

The wheel lurched into motion, carrying us upward. Yulia's hand gripped the safety bar, her knuckles white. Without thinking, I covered her hand with mine. She tensed, then slowly turned her palm upward, our fingers intertwining.

"Been a while since we've done something like this," I said, my voice low. "Just the three of us."

She nodded, her eyes fixed on the horizon as we rose higher. "It's nice. We should do it more often."

Our car reached the top, swaying gently as the wheel stopped to let more passengers on below. The fairgrounds spread out beneath us, a swirl of movement and color. In the distance, I could see the compound, a dark smudge against the landscape. Two worlds, so close yet so different.

Yulia followed my gaze. "You're thinking about the club?"

"No." I squeezed her hand gently. "I'm thinking about you."

Her gaze snapped to mine, wide and startled.

"Salvation," she whispered, my road name on her lips sending a shiver down my spine.

The wheel jerked back into motion, breaking the moment. She pulled her hand from mine, tucking it safely in her lap as we descended. Below, I could see Clover in her car, trying to watch us with undisguised interest.

When we reached the bottom, the operator unlatched our safety bar. "You folks have a good time now," he called as we exited. "Ain't often I see a family so happy together."

Clover appeared at my side, grinning from ear to ear. "See? Even he thinks you two should get a room."

"Clover!" Yulia gasped.

I placed a hand on my daughter's shoulder, squeezing just firmly enough to communicate my warning. "Enough of that."

But Clover just laughed, unrepentant. "What? I'm just saying what everyone's thinking." She skipped ahead a few steps, then turned, walking backward to face us. "What's next? Tilt-A-Whirl? Bumper cars?"

I glanced at Yulia, finding her gaze already on me. Something had shifted between us, some invisible boundary crossed. The thought terrified and exhilarated me in equal measure.

"Your choice," I told her, voice pitched low enough that only she could hear.

Her smile, small and secret, was like the sun breaking through clouds. "Bumper cars," she decided. "I want to see if your driving is any better there than on the road."

Clover whooped and took off toward the ride, leaving us to follow at our own pace. This time, when my hand found the small of Yulia's back, neither of us pretended it was just about navigating the crowd.

We spent the next two hours going from ride to ride and playing a few games. I was getting exhausted and ready to head home.

"Please, Dad? I've been on it three times with you guys already." Clover's eyes, so like her mother's, pleaded with me. We stood at the entrance to the Screamer, the roller coaster she'd been eyeing since we arrived. "I want to ride by myself this time. I'm not a baby."

I crossed my arms, scanning the crowd around us -- an old habit that never died. "You're sixteen."

"Exactly!" She bounced on her toes. "Practically an adult."

Yulia touched my arm lightly, her fingers warm through my T-shirt. "Let her go. We'll wait right here."

I frowned, caught between my instinct to protect and the knowledge that I needed to give Clover room to grow. "Fine. One ride. Then we find something to eat."

Clover's face split into a grin. She squeezed my arm, then darted toward the entrance, her dark hair streaming behind her. I watched until she disappeared into the line, unease settling in my gut like a stone.

"She'll be fine," Yulia said softly beside me. "The line wraps around. We can see her from that bench."

She nodded toward an empty spot near a popcorn vendor. I grunted in agreement, and we made our way over.

We sat close together on the bench, my thigh brushing against hers. The roller coaster's chain clanked as cars climbed the first hill, followed by screams as they plunged down the other side. I kept my gaze on the line, picking out Clover's familiar figure as she inched closer to the front.

"Hungry?" Yulia asked, breaking the comfortable silence between us.

I realized I was starving. "Yeah. Popcorn?"

She nodded, and I stood, crossing to the nearby vendor. I returned a minute later with a large bag, settling back beside her -- closer than before, though neither of us acknowledged it.

I held the bag between us. Yulia reached in, her fingers brushing against mine as we both grabbed for popcorn at the same time. Unlike earlier, neither of us pulled away immediately. The contact lingered, deliberate now.

"Sorry," she murmured, not sounding sorry at all.

"Don't be." I let my fingers slide against hers before withdrawing, heat crawling up my neck.

We ate in silence for a moment, both of us watching the roller coaster and pretending that's all we were focused on. She laughed at something and the sound wrapped around me like a physical touch.

"Your accent," I said without thinking. "It gets stronger when you're happy and when you're nervous."

"You'd think after all this time it would be gone."

"Not gone." I shook my head. "Just… softer. Except when you're emotional."

"You've been paying attention." Her voice was quiet, almost wondering.

I looked at her then, really looked at her. The woman beside me was so different from the broken girl

I'd married to protect. Her eyes, once vacant with despair, now held a quiet confidence. The hesitant way she'd moved, always braced for pain, had given way to a grace that drew my eye whenever she entered a room.

"Yeah," I admitted. "I have."

She ducked her head, a smile playing at the corners of her mouth as she reached for more popcorn.

"She's growing up so fast," Yulia said, nodding toward where Clover now stood near the front of the line. "Almost a woman."

I grunted, not ready to acknowledge that reality. "Too fast."

"You can't keep her at the compound forever, you know." Yulia's voice was gentle but firm. "College is only two years away."

The thought sat like lead in my stomach.

"Cyclops' kids stayed close. Not all will." She shifted beside me, her shoulder pressing against mine. "She has dreams. Big ones."

"I know." I did know. I'd heard Clover talking about universities on the east coast, about traveling abroad. Each conversation had felt like a knife twisting in my gut. "I just worry."

"About what she'll face out there? Or about being left behind?"

The question hit too close to home. I stared at the roller coaster, watching as the next group of riders was secured into their seats. "Both, I guess."

Yulia's hand settled on my forearm, her touch featherlight. "You've given her a good life, Salvation. A safe one. That's more than most can say."

I turned to face her, struck by the certainty in her voice. "We both have," I corrected. "Don't sell yourself short, Yulia. You've been as much a parent to her as I have."

Something flickered in her eyes -- surprise, maybe, or gratitude. "I've tried. She made it easy to love her."

"Like her mom that way," I said, the old grief a dull ache now, not the sharp pain it once was. "Carina had that same quality."

Yulia nodded, her fingers tracing absent patterns on my arm. The touch sent heat spiraling through me. "Clover talks about her sometimes. Asks me questions."

"What kind of questions?"

"If I think Carina would be proud of her. If she looks like her." Yulia's eyes met mine. "If you still miss her."

My throat tightened. "What do you tell her?"

"That of course Carina would be proud. That yes, she has her mother's eyes and smile." She paused, her gaze dropping to where her fingers still rested on my arm. "And that missing someone doesn't mean you can't move forward."

The words hung between us, loaded with meaning. Around us, the fair continued its chaotic dance -- children laughing, barkers calling, music blaring from rides. But in our small bubble on the bench, the world had narrowed to just us two.

"Yulia," I began, my voice rougher than intended. "About the other night --"

"I know." She lifted her gaze to mine, something vulnerable and brave in her expression. "We need to talk."

"Yeah." I shifted closer, the popcorn forgotten between us. "But maybe we need to do more than talk."

Her breath caught. The air between us seemed to

thicken, charged with eleven years of unspoken feelings. Slowly, giving her every chance to pull away, I raised my hand to her face. My thumb brushed across her cheekbone, and her eyes fluttered shut at the touch.

"Salvation," she whispered, leaning slightly toward me.

I closed the distance between us, drawn by a force I'd been fighting too long. Her breath, warm and sweet, mingled with mine as our lips hovered a hairsbreadth apart --

"That was awesome!"

Clover's voice shattered the moment. We jerked apart, Yulia nearly knocking over the popcorn as she straightened. My daughter bounded up to us, hair windblown, cheeks flushed with excitement.

"Did you see that last drop? I had my hands up the whole time!" She flopped onto the bench beside me, oblivious to what she'd interrupted. "Can we get something to eat? I'm starving."

I cleared my throat, struggling to shift mental gears. "Sure. What do you want?"

"Corn dogs. No, funnel cake. No, wait -- both!" She jumped up again, energy seemingly inexhaustible.

I glanced at Yulia, finding her cheeks flushed, eyes bright with what might have been disappointment or anticipation. When our gazes locked, a silent promise passed between us: Later. We *would* finish this later.

"Come on, slowpokes!" Clover called, already several steps ahead.

I stood, offering my hand to Yulia. After a moment's hesitation, she took it, her fingers sliding between mine as if they belonged there. Neither of us let go as we followed my daughter into the crowd.

* * *

I felt the satisfied fatigue of a night well spent with the two people who mattered most. I caught Yulia's eye as Clover examined a henna tattoo stand, and the small smile she gave me sent warmth spreading through my chest. Later, I promised myself. We'd finish what we started.

"We should head back," I said, checking my watch. "It's getting late."

Clover groaned, clutching the oversized tiger I'd won her at the shooting gallery. "Just one more ride? Please?"

"Tomorrow," I promised. "Fair's here all weekend."

"Fine," she sighed dramatically, then brightened. "But we're definitely coming back."

Yulia laughed, the sound lighter than I'd heard in years. "Of course we are. Your father still needs to prove he can handle the Tilt-A-Whirl without turning green."

"That was the Gravitron, not the Tilt-A-Whirl," I grumbled, but couldn't keep the smile from my face. Something had shifted between us today -- walls coming down, possibilities opening up. The thought made my heart beat faster.

We started toward the exit, the fairgrounds now more crowded than before as teens and adults poured in for the final evening shows. Colored lights blinked overhead, casting moving shadows across the packed dirt paths. Clover walked ahead as she pointed out things she wanted to try tomorrow. Yulia walked beside me, close enough that our hands brushed occasionally. Each touch sent electricity racing up my arm.

"Today was nice," she said.

"Yeah," I agreed, wanting to say more but not

finding the words. Not here, surrounded by strangers. "It was."

My phone vibrated in my pocket. I pulled it out, recognizing Beast's number on the screen. A text message glowed in the gathering darkness: *Need you back at compound. Trouble with the Diablos. How soon can you get here*?

I frowned, reading it twice. The Diablos were a small-time gang who'd been making noise about expanding into our territory for the last six months. Nothing serious yet, but Beast wouldn't text unless it needed attention.

"Everything okay?" Yulia asked, noticing my expression.

"Yeah, just club business." I typed a quick response: *Heading back now. 30 minutes.*

I slipped the phone back into my pocket and looked up, ready to call Clover back from where she'd wandered ahead.

She wasn't there.

I scanned the crowd, expecting to spot her dark hair, the ridiculous tiger. Nothing.

"Clover?" I called, stepping forward. "Where'd she go?"

Yulia moved to my side. "She was just ahead of us. Maybe she stopped at one of the booths?"

I looked to my right, where a row of food vendors lined the path. No sign of her. To my left, more game booths, all packed with fairgoers, none of them my daughter.

"I'll check this way," Yulia said, already moving toward the food stands. "She probably got hungry again."

I nodded, heading toward the games, my eyes searching for Clover's familiar form. The crowd seemed to thicken, bodies pressing against me as I pushed through, calling her name. Carnival music blared from all directions, drowning out my voice. Sweat beaded on my forehead despite the cooling evening air.

After checking three game booths with no success, I turned back toward where I'd left Yulia. She'd be searching the food stands, and maybe Clover had already found her way back to our meeting spot. When we'd first arrived, I'd made sure to set up a place in case we got separated. I quickened my pace, shoving more forcefully through the crowd.

But when I reached the place where I'd last seen Yulia, she wasn't there.

A cold knot formed in my stomach. "Yulia?" I called, louder than before. A few people glanced my way, but most ignored me, too wrapped up in their own fair experiences.

I pulled out my phone, dialing Yulia's number. It rang four times, then went to voicemail. I tried Clover next. Same result.

"Fuck," I muttered, earning a glare from a nearby mother with small children.

I moved methodically, checking each food stand, each game booth, retracing our steps to rides we'd enjoyed earlier. With each empty search, the knot in my stomach tightened. Ten minutes became fifteen. My calls went straight to voicemail now, both phones apparently off or dead.

"Have you seen a teenage girl, dark hair, about this tall?" I asked a cotton candy vendor. "Or a woman, dark blonde hair, slight accent? They were here twenty minutes ago."

The woman shook her head, already turning to her next customer.

I kept moving, kept searching, but a sickening certainty was building inside me. This wasn't just getting separated in a crowd. Something was wrong.

Years of club life had honed my instincts, trained me to recognize threats before they fully materialized. Those instincts were screaming now. I returned to our last meeting spot, scanning the area with new eyes. Looking for signs I might have missed.

That's when I saw it -- a small slip of paper partially hidden under a discarded popcorn box. I wouldn't have noticed it if not for the corner that peeked out -- paper too white, too clean to be regular trash. I bent down and picked it up, unfolding it carefully.

Two words, written in neat block letters: FOUND YOU.

The blood in my veins turned to ice. Yulia's past. Her father's enemies. The people we'd been protecting her from for eleven years. They'd found us.

I crumpled the paper in my fist, panic clawing up my throat. My eyes swept the crowd again, this time looking not for my family but for watchers. For men who didn't belong. For threats I should have seen coming.

How long had they been following us? Days? Weeks? Had they been waiting for the perfect opportunity -- a moment when we were relaxed, in public, surrounded by civilians?

I dialed Beast's number with shaking fingers.

"Yeah?" His gruff voice answered on the second ring.

"They're gone," I said, my voice tight with controlled fear. "Yulia and Clover. They're gone."

A beat of silence. Then: "What happened?"

I explained in clipped sentences, ending with the

note. "It's them, Beast. The Russians. They've found her."

"Where are you exactly?" His voice had shifted, all business now.

I gave him the location, describing landmarks near where I stood.

"Stay put. We're on our way. All of us." I heard him barking orders in the background. "Five minutes, brother. Don't do anything stupid."

"They have my family," I growled, desperation making my voice shake.

"I know. And we'll get them back." His tone brooked no argument. "But we do it smart. Together. Five minutes."

The call ended. I stood rooted to the spot, my heart pounding so hard it hurt. Around me, the fair continued its cheerful chaos -- lights spinning, music blaring, people laughing. The contrast to the horror unfolding in my life was unbearable.

Five minutes stretched like an eternity. I scanned every face that passed, memorizing features, looking for anyone watching me too closely. The note burned in my clenched fist. FOUND YOU. Two words that destroyed the life we'd built. Two words that threatened everything I loved.

The first motorcycle engines reached my ears three minutes later, a low rumble growing louder as they approached the fairground entrance. People turned to look, murmuring as leather-clad men appeared at the edge of the crowd, moving with purpose.

Beast reached me first, Hawk and Crow flanking him. More brothers followed -- Brick, Forge, at least six others. Their faces were grim, hands hovering near concealed weapons.

"Any contact?" Beast asked without preamble.

I shook my head, handing him the crumpled note. "Nothing since this."

He read it, jaw tightening. "We've got guys watching all exits. No one matching their description has left the fairgrounds." He gripped my shoulder, his eyes hard. "We'll find them, Salvation."

But as I stood amid the swirling fair lights, surrounded by my brothers, all I could think was that I'd failed. Failed to protect the two people who mattered most. Failed to see the danger until it was too late.

"They'll want to take her back to Russia," I said, my voice hollow. "Finish what they started all those years ago."

"And Clover?" Hawk asked quietly. "Why would they want her? I'm not sure this is the Russians."

The question hit me like a physical blow. Clover was collateral damage -- an innocent caught in a war that had nothing to do with her. What would they do with a witness? A sixteen-year-old girl who could identify them? As to his other question, it had to be the Russians. Who else would target Yulia?

"We need to move," I said, panic surging fresh. "Now."

Beast nodded, already directing brothers to search patterns. As they dispersed into the crowd, a terrible certainty settled in my gut. This wasn't a simple case of getting separated. This was the beginning of a nightmare I'd spent eleven years trying to prevent.

And as the colorful lights spun around me, as families laughed and children squealed on rides, all I could think was: *I should have seen it coming.*

Chapter Four

Yulia

Pain pulsed behind my eyes, a steady throb that dragged me from the darkness into unwelcome consciousness. I tried to lift my hand to my head but found my wrists bound together with something tight that bit into my skin. Panic flared, momentarily overriding the pain. My eyes snapped open to darkness, then adjusted to reveal dim shadows cast by a single flickering bulb hanging from a concrete ceiling. This wasn't the fair. This wasn't home. Cold dread settled in my stomach as memories flashed -- cotton candy, colored lights, Salvation's warm gaze just before we lost Clover in the crowd. Before everything went black.

Clover. My heartbeat accelerated. Where was she?

I forced myself to sit up despite the way the room tilted around me. The damp and cold from the concrete floor seeped through my jeans. Concrete walls surrounded us in a small, windowless box. A basement, maybe. Or a storage room. I scanned the space and my breath caught when I spotted a small figure huddled against the wall.

"Clover?" My voice came out as a rasp, my throat raw as if I'd been screaming.

She lifted her head, face pale in the weak light. Zip ties bound her wrists together in front of her, matching mine. Her eyes were red-rimmed, mascara streaked down her cheeks, but she wasn't crying now. She stared at me with a shell-shocked expression that broke my heart.

"Yulia," she whispered. "You're awake."

I scooted toward her, ignoring the wave of nausea that followed the movement. "Are you hurt?"

"Just scared. I never should have gone back to that henna booth. They grabbed me while I was looking at the tattoos and deciding if I wanted one. Put something over my mouth. Then not much later, they took you too." Her voice cracked. "They dragged you into the van and took off."

I reached out with my bound hands, brushing hair from her face. My fingers trembled slightly. "I'm sorry I couldn't protect you."

"Not your fault," she murmured, leaning into my touch like she had as a small child. Despite everything, my heart swelled with love for this girl who wasn't mine by blood but was mine in every way that mattered.

The Bratva. It had to be. After eleven years, they'd finally found me. My father's enemies, coming to finish what they'd started when I was sixteen. I traced one of the silvery scars on my wrist with my thumb, the familiar gesture bringing no comfort now. I'd always known this day might come, had prepared myself for it, but I'd never imagined they'd take Clover too.

"It will be okay, *malishka*," I whispered, my accent thickening as it always did under stress. "Your father will find us."

"How?" Her voice was so small, so afraid.

"He's Salvation." I tried to sound confident. "And the entire club will be looking. The Reckless Kings do not abandon their own."

Clover nodded, pressing closer to my side. I wrapped my bound arms around her as best I could, ignoring the bite of the plastic ties. We sat in silence for several minutes, listening to the distant hum of what might have been a furnace or water heater.

Then, voices filtered through the thin door -- men arguing. I stiffened, straining to hear.

"-- too fucking low," one voice snarled. "They can afford more. They got the whole drug trade locked down."

"Don't be stupid," a second voice replied. "Two hundred grand is plenty. Push for more and they'll just come gunning for us."

"That's the whole point of hostages, dipshit. Insurance."

"These ain't just any hostages. That's Salvation's kid. And his woman."

"Exactly. Time to teach those Reckless Kings a lesson in humility. They walk around like they own this town."

I frowned, confusion replacing some of my fear. These weren't Russian accents. There was no mention of my father, of taking me back to face punishment. Just talk of ransom and teaching the club a lesson.

The realization hit me like ice water. These weren't Bratva professionals sent to collect me. They were local thugs who'd targeted the club, and Clover and I had been convenient targets at the fair.

Relief made me dizzy for a moment -- relief that this wasn't about my past. But it was quickly replaced by new fear. Amateur kidnappers were unpredictable. Dangerous in different ways than trained Bratva soldiers would be.

"Two hundred thousand, final offer," the second voice continued. "We'll be in touch in the next hour, give them proof of life, and set the drop for midnight."

"That's not much time. What about six in the morning?"

"I guess that works," the second voice said.

"Fine. But I still say --"

The voices faded as the men moved away from the door. I looked down at Clover, who had gone very still against me.

"They want money," she whispered. "Dad won't give it to them, will he?"

I shook my head slightly. "No, *malishka*. The club doesn't pay ransoms." I kept my voice steady, though my heart raced. "But that doesn't mean they won't come for us."

Clover trembled against me, and I felt wetness on my arm where her face pressed. Silent tears. I shifted to pull her closer, shielding her with my body as if I could somehow absorb her fear.

"Do not cry, little one," I murmured, pressing my lips to the top of her head. "We will be strong, yes? For your father."

She nodded against my shoulder, but her tears continued to fall, soaking into my shirt. I held her tighter, my mind racing. They would call the club. Make demands. Show proof that we were alive. And Salvation… what would he do? I knew him well enough to know he wouldn't sit and wait. Wouldn't follow their instructions. He would come for us with the fury of a storm, bringing the entire club with him.

And these men -- these stupid, amateur kidnappers -- had no idea what they'd unleashed.

I stroked Clover's hair, whispering reassurances in a mix of English and Russian, while part of my mind calculated. How long had we been here? How long would it take the club to track us? What would our captors do when they realized their mistake?

Footsteps approached the door again. I tensed, angling my body to keep Clover behind me as the lock rattled. Whatever happened next, I would protect her. This girl who had become my daughter in all but blood. This child who had helped heal my broken pieces over the years.

I was Bratva born, and now I was a Reckless King's woman. These men would learn there were fates worse than dealing with the club. They would learn what happened when they threatened a mother's child. I'd been weak and defenseless before. Now I had a true reason to fight, and I'd give them hell if they tried to hurt Clover.

The door began to open, and I narrowed my eyes against the sudden light, keeping my body between Clover and whatever came through that door.

It swung open with a rusty creak, flooding our dim prison with harsh fluorescent light from the hallway beyond. Two men filled the doorway -- the smaller one flicking a wall switch that brought our single bulb to full strength, temporarily blinding me. I blinked away the spots in my vision, taking their measure as they stepped inside. Not Bratva. Not professionals. Just local trash who'd made the worst mistake of their lives.

The taller one stood in front with a lazy confidence that marked him as the leader. Lanky but wiry, with dirty blond hair pulled back in a greasy ponytail. His most distinctive feature was the tattoo that slithered up his neck -- a green and black snake that curved from beneath his collar to behind his ear. Cheap work, prison-done from the look of it. His companion was shorter but broader, muscles straining the seams of his T-shirt. His head was cleanly shaved, with a jagged scar bisecting one eyebrow.

Snake Tattoo carried a plastic bag in one hand and a smartphone in the other. He tossed the bag at my feet, where it landed with a soft thud. Through the thin plastic, I could make out the shapes of water bottles and fast-food containers.

"Dinner time, ladies," he said, his voice matching the one I'd heard through the door. "Don't say we don't treat our guests right."

Behind me, Clover shifted closer, her fingers digging into my arm hard enough to bruise. I welcomed the pain -- it helped me focus, kept the fear at bay.

"What do you want from us?" I asked.

Snake Tattoo smirked. "Just a little insurance while your biker buddies put together our money. Nothing personal." He glanced at his shorter companion. "Isn't that right, Marco?"

The shorter man -- Marco -- grunted, his gaze darting nervously around the room rather than looking directly at us. "Let's just get this done, Vince."

I filed away the names. Vince and Marco. Amateurs who hadn't even thought to hide their identities. They were already dead men walking -- they just didn't know it yet.

Vince held up his phone. "Time for your close-up. Gotta show the Reckless Kings that their precious family is still breathing."

"My dad will kill you for this," Clover said, her voice surprisingly steady despite the fear I could feel trembling through her body. "All of them will."

Vince barked out a laugh. "Hear that, Marco? Little girl's making threats." He pointed the phone at us, the small light beside the camera illuminating. "Smile for Daddy, sweetheart. Tell him how well we're treating you."

Clover's grip on my arm tightened. "My dad will come for us," she repeated, staring directly into the camera. "The whole club will."

"Yeah, yeah. That's the idea." Vince moved closer, his phone focused on our faces. "They'll come with our money, and you'll go home in one piece. Simple business transaction."

I kept my face expressionless, evaluating our options. Both men appeared to be armed -- bulges at their waistbands suggesting concealed handguns. The zip ties bit into my wrists, too tight to slip free without tearing my skin open. Not yet. Not with Clover to protect.

"Say something," Vince snapped, annoyance flashing across his face. "Need to prove you're both alive and kicking."

"I still say we should just use pictures," the other one grumbled. Vince sighed and took a few pictures, then glared at the man as if to ask *happy now*? Then he turned back to face me, pointing the phone my way again.

I met Vince's gaze steadily. "We're alive. For now."

He sneered, stepping closer. "Not very cooperative, are you? Maybe we need to be more convincing." He reached out suddenly, fingers gripping my chin and forcing my face toward the camera. His nails dug into my skin. "Say hello to your old man, Russian. Tell him to have our money ready."

I stared directly into the lens, imagining Salvation watching this footage. Imagining his rage, his fear, his determination. I wanted him to see that I wasn't broken. That I would protect Clover with my life. That I believed in him.

"We are unharmed," I said clearly, my blue eyes never wavering from the camera. "Do not worry about us, Salvation."

The message was clear. *Do not pay. Do not follow their instructions. Come for us your way.*

Vince released my chin with a small shove, seemingly satisfied. "See? Was that so hard?" He turned the camera toward Clover. "Your turn, kid."

Clover glanced at me, then lifted her chin in a gesture so reminiscent of her father that my heart clenched. "I'm okay, Dad. Don't worry about me."

Vince lowered the phone, tapping at the screen. "That ought to do it. Proof of life, check. Ransom demand, coming up next." He glanced at his watch. "They've got enough time to get the money together."

Marco shifted uncomfortably by the door. "We should get going. Make the call from somewhere else. Or better yet, just send a note. Pay someone to deliver it."

"Relax," Vince said, pocketing his phone. "No one's tracking us here."

Marco's gaze darted to me, then away. "I don't like this, man. The Russian especially. You hear what they say about the club's connections?"

I kept my expression neutral, though a small thrill ran through me. The club's reputation preceded them, even among these lowlifes.

Vince rolled his eyes. "They're just women. The club will pay to get them back, end of story."

"The younger one is his kid. The older one's his wife," Marco persisted. "What if they've got ties to the real Russians? The serious ones?"

A cold smile touched my lips before I could suppress it. Marco saw it and took a step back.

"See? She's fucking smiling, man." His voice rose slightly. "This isn't right."

Vince turned to me, irritation plain on his face. "Something funny?"

I shrugged as best I could with my bound hands. "Just thinking about what Salvation will do when he finds you."

"If," Vince corrected, but I noted the flicker of uncertainty in his eyes. "If he finds us. And he won't, not before we get our money and disappear." He nodded toward the bag at my feet. "Eat up. Might be a while before your next meal."

He backed toward the door, keeping his eyes on us. Marco was already halfway into the hallway, clearly eager to be gone.

"Don't try anything stupid," Vince warned as he reached the threshold. "We'll be right outside. And we won't be as nice next time."

The door slammed shut behind them. The lock clicked, followed by the sound of retreating footsteps.

Clover exhaled shakily against my shoulder. "Did I do okay?"

I turned to her, examining her face in the harsh light. Despite her fear, there was a determination in her eyes that reminded me so much of Salvation it made my chest ache.

"You did perfectly, *malishka*," I murmured, pressing my forehead briefly against hers. "Your father will be very proud."

"They're idiots," she whispered, glancing nervously at the door.

I nodded, reaching for the bag of food with my bound hands. "Yes. And that may save us -- or condemn them." I managed a small, reassuring smile. "Either way, we must keep our strength up."

As Clover helped me open the water bottles with our awkward, bound hands, I kept my ear tuned to the sounds outside our prison. Waiting. Planning. Preparing for whatever came next.

Their footsteps faded down the hallway, followed by the muffled sound of another door closing. I waited, counting to thirty in my head before moving. We might not get another chance to be alone, and I needed to know exactly what we were dealing with. I pushed myself to my feet, ignoring the way my head throbbed, and began a methodical inspection of our prison, taking in details I'd missed in the initial panic of waking up bound and disoriented. Clover watched me from the floor, her eyes tracking my movements as I tested the walls, examined the door, and assessed everything that might become a weapon or an escape route.

"What are you doing?" she whispered, scooting back against the wall to give me space.

"Looking for anything useful," I replied, keeping my voice low. "Anything that might help us."

The room was small, maybe twelve feet square. Concrete walls, concrete floor. A single metal door with a deadbolt lock -- simple, but effective. No windows. The only light came from the bare bulb hanging from the ceiling, too high to reach even if I jumped. A dirty mattress had been tossed in one corner -- the one we'd been sitting on. In the opposite corner sat a plastic bucket -- our bathroom, presumably. How thoughtful.

My gaze traveled upward, following a network of pipes that ran along the ceiling. Water pipes, maybe, or heating. They disappeared into the wall opposite the door. A basement or utility room, as I'd suspected.

"Anything?" Clover asked, hope tinging her voice.

I shook my head, frustration gnawing at me. "Not yet."

I moved to the door, examining it more carefully.

Solid metal, hinges on the outside where we couldn't reach them. The lock appeared sturdy. I pressed my ear against the cold surface, listening for any sounds that might tell us more about where we were. Faintly, I could hear a mechanical hum -- a furnace or water heater -- and distant voices, too muffled to make out words.

Returning to Clover, I sank down beside her on the mattress and held up my bound wrists, examining the zip ties. They were pulled tight, biting into my skin. Not impossibly tight, but enough that I couldn't simply slip free. I twisted my wrists experimentally, testing the give of the plastic.

"Can you get them off?" Clover asked, watching intently.

"Not easily." I glanced at her bonds. "They're amateurs, *malishka*. Professional kidnappers would have used something stronger. Or kept us separate. Left a guard. These men are trusting us to stay put and not fight back."

Her eyes widened slightly. "How do you know what professional kidnappers do?"

I paused, considering how much to tell her. She knew pieces of my past -- the boarding school, the rescue by the club, my marriage to her father for protection. But not everything. Not the darkest parts.

"I grew up around dangerous men," I said finally. "My father's associates. I learned things, even as a child. What to watch for. How to survive." I nodded toward the door. "These men? They're not professionals. They're local thugs who think they can make easy money."

"Will Dad pay them?" Her voice was small, uncertain.

I met her gaze steadily. "No, *malishka*. The club

doesn't pay ransoms."

Fear flashed across her face. "Then what --"

"Shh." I moved closer, lowering my voice to barely above a whisper. "Your father won't pay them. Neither will the club. That's not how the Reckless Kings operate."

"But then how will we --"

"They will come for us," I continued, certainty hardening my voice. "Your father, Beast, all of them. They won't follow the kidnappers' instructions, won't play by their rules. They will hunt them down and destroy them completely."

Clover's eyes widened. "Destroy them?"

"These men made a fatal mistake taking us," I said, not softening the truth. She'd grown up in the club. She knew what they were capable of. "The Reckless Kings protect their own. And they make examples of those who threaten what's theirs."

A small shiver ran through her, but she nodded. "Dad will come."

"Yes. And we must be ready when he does." I glanced down at our bound wrists. "We should conserve our strength. Eat what they brought us. Stay alert. Look for any opportunity."

Clover reached for the fast-food bag with her bound hands, her movements awkward but determined. We ate in silence, the cold burgers tasteless but necessary fuel. I made her drink an entire bottle of water, knowing dehydration would only make things worse.

"What do you think they'll do?" she asked after a while, her voice steadier now. "When they realize the club won't pay?"

I considered the question carefully. "They'll get desperate. Desperate men make mistakes." I met her eyes. "That's when we'll have our chance."

"What if they..." She trailed off, unable to voice her fears.

I leaned forward, pressing my forehead against hers as I had done countless times since she was a child. "Listen to me, Clover. I will not let anyone hurt you. Do you understand? Not ever."

She nodded, swallowing hard. "I know."

"Your father taught me many things over the years," I continued, a small smile touching my lips. "How to shoot. How to fight. How to survive." I didn't add that these lessons had built on what I'd already learned growing up in the shadows of the Bratva, as that hadn't done me any good when monsters actually threatened me. But I wasn't that weak teenager anymore. "If those men come through that door intending harm, they will regret it."

Something shifted in Clover's expression -- fear giving way to a tentative confidence. She was Salvation's daughter, after all. Courage ran in her blood.

"What can I do?" she asked. "To help?"

Pride swelled in my chest. "Stay close to me. Follow my lead. And if I tell you to run, you run. No arguments."

She nodded solemnly. "Okay."

We fell silent again, listening to the distant sounds of the building. My mind turned to Salvation, imagining him watching the video our captors had sent. Seeing the defiance in my eyes. Understanding my message. By now, the club would be mobilized, hunting through the city for any trace of us. For any connection to Vince and Marco.

I allowed myself a small, cold smile as I pictured the look on Snake Tattoo's face when he realized his mistake. When he understood exactly who he'd taken and what it meant for him. The Reckless Kings were dangerous enough on an ordinary day. But Salvation, when his family was threatened? There would be no mercy. No quarter given.

The thought should have disturbed me. Once, perhaps, it would have. But eleven years with the club had changed me. Mothering Clover had changed me. Loving Salvation -- first from a distance, then with growing certainty -- had changed me. I no longer flinched from the darkness.

A sudden noise from beyond the door snapped me back to the present. Footsteps approaching again, heavier this time. Angry. I tensed, rising to my feet in one fluid motion.

"Behind me," I murmured to Clover, positioning myself between her and the door.

She scrambled up, pressing close to my back. I could feel her trembling, but her voice was steady when she whispered, "Be careful."

The lock rattled. I widened my stance, centering my weight. With my hands bound, my options were limited, but not nonexistent. I'd survived worse situations than this. And I had more to fight for now than I ever had before.

The door began to open, and I steeled myself, ready to protect my daughter at any cost. These men had made the biggest mistake of their lives taking us. And whether Salvation reached us first or we freed ourselves, one thing was certain…

They would pay for it in blood.

Chapter Five

Salvation

I barely felt my hands on the steering wheel as I roared through the gates of the compound, my truck fishtailing on the gravel. The world had narrowed to a single burning point of focus since the moment Yulia and Clover disappeared from the fairgrounds. Every second that passed without finding them felt like a knife twisting deeper into my chest, the edges of my vision tinged red with a fury I could barely contain.

The truck skidded to a halt in front of the clubhouse, dust billowing around me like a storm cloud. I threw the door open and stepped out, scanning the compound with hawk-like intensity. An hour of searching the fairgrounds with my brothers had yielded nothing. I'd had a growing sense of dread that clawed at my insides.

Of course, Hawk had pointed out that we had no idea if that note was intended for my family or was merely a coincidence. Maybe what I saw as a sinister message was a teenager's playful prank on a friend.

A Prospect -- Decker, the newest kid -- jogged toward me, his face pale under his week-old scruff. Something in my expression made him slow his approach, caution replacing urgency in his steps.

"Salvation," he called, stopping several feet away. His Adam's apple bobbed as he swallowed. "I was about to call you."

"What is it?" My voice came out flat, stripped of emotion I couldn't afford to show.

Decker shifted his weight, glancing over his shoulder toward the clubhouse. "A kid came by about twenty minutes ago. Dropped off a note. We had an issue at the gate right after and I forgot about it." He pulled an envelope from his cut. "Said it was for you specifically."

My blood turned to ice. I closed the distance between us in two strides and snatched the envelope from his hand. "What kid? Who sent him?"

"Just some neighborhood boy, maybe ten years old. I'm not good at guessing ages. They all look fucking small to me." Decker took a step back, hands raising slightly. "Said someone gave him five bucks to deliver it. Couldn't describe who paid him -- just said it was a man in a baseball cap who stopped him near the convenience store on Fourth."

My fingers trembled as I tore open the envelope, the roaring in my ears drowning out everything but the frantic hammering of my heart. Inside was a single folded sheet of notebook paper, the kind you'd find in any school kid's backpack. I unfolded it, a muscle in my jaw twitching as I forced myself to read the blocky, handwritten text.

SALVATION --

WE HAVE YOUR WIFE AND KID. THEY'RE ALIVE FOR NOW. $200,000 BY 6AM OR THAT CHANGES. WAIT FOR INSTRUCTIONS. NO COPS OR THEY DIE.

A photo was stapled to the bottom of the page -- Yulia and Clover, bound with zip ties, sitting against a concrete wall. Their faces were pale but composed, defiance rather than fear in their eyes. The sight simultaneously relieved me -- they were alive -- and unleashed a wave of rage so intense my vision blurred.

"Is it…" Decker began, then fell silent when I raised my gaze to his.

My hands clenched so tight around the paper

that it crumpled, knuckles going white with strain. A coldness settled over me, something deeper and more dangerous than the hot fury that had driven me since the fairgrounds. This was the calm that came before violence, the still water that hid deadly currents.

"Get Beast," I said, my voice so controlled it barely sounded like my own. "Tell him I need everyone. Now."

Decker nodded rapidly, backing away. "He's already inside with Hawk and Shield. They're setting up Church. Said something about turning it into a war room."

I folded the note carefully, tucking it into my cut, right above my heart. The photo I kept in my hand, my thumb rubbing over Yulia's face. The hard, determined set of her jaw. The way she'd positioned herself slightly in front of Clover. Protective. Fierce. My woman. My daughter.

Something shifted in my chest. Eleven years we'd been married on paper, living under the same roof, raising Clover together. Eleven years of respecting boundaries, of friendship that had slowly, inexorably deepened into something more. And now, when we'd finally been ready to acknowledge what had been building between us for so long, they'd been ripped away from me.

The Prospect still hovered nearby, watching me warily like you'd watch a feral dog that might lunge without warning.

"You said a kid delivered this?" I asked, forcing the words past the tightness in my throat.

Decker nodded. "Yeah, couldn't have been more than ten. Skinny little thing with glasses. Said he didn't know what was in it, just that he got five bucks to bring it here."

I nodded once, digesting this. Amateurs, then. Professionals wouldn't have used a local kid as a messenger. Wouldn't have left a paper trail. That was both good and bad news. Amateurs were unpredictable, prone to panic, but they also made mistakes. Mistakes I could exploit.

"Did anyone follow the kid? See where he went?"

"Brick tried but lost him in the neighborhoods past Main. Kid knew the alleys better."

A muscle twitched in my cheek as I tamped down a surge of frustration. "Tell Beast I'm coming. And find Shield. I need him working on this now."

"Already on it." Decker jerked his head toward the clubhouse. "He's set up in the new tech room. Been monitoring traffic cams since you called from the fair."

I headed into the clubhouse, each step measured, controlled. The Prospect trailed a few steps behind me, giving me space. Smart kid. He'd noticed what the others would soon see -- that something fundamental had changed in me since leaving the fairgrounds. The desperate fear had crystallized into something harder, colder. More lethal.

They wanted money. Two hundred thousand by six in the morning. Not a lot of time to get it together. But money wasn't what they'd get from me. No, they'd made their final mistake the moment they put their hands on Yulia and Clover.

I reached the clubhouse steps, pausing to look back at the compound. At the life we'd built here. The home we'd made. My family wasn't defined by blood or legal documents, but by the bonds we'd forged through years of trust and loyalty. By the love that had grown between us, spoken or not.

I would find them. I would bring them home.

And then I would make those responsible wish they'd never been born.

That wasn't a promise. It was a fact, as inevitable as the setting sun.

* * *

Church felt smaller than usual, the air heavy with cigarette smoke and tension. Maps of the city covered the table, streets marked in red where brothers had already searched, yellow highlighting possible areas still to cover. Empty coffee cups and crushed beer cans littered every empty surface, evidence of the hours that had passed since the fair. Since my family had vanished. I closed the door behind me.

Beast stood at the head of the table, arms crossed over his chest, his face carved from stone. The President's patch on his cut seemed to gleam under the harsh fluorescent lighting, a reminder of the power he wielded, the resources at his command. Hawk leaned against the wall to my right, his usual easy posture replaced by coiled tension, like a spring wound too tight.

"Let me see it," Beast said, extending his hand.

I pulled the crumpled note from my cut and passed it to him, holding onto the photo. Some things were too personal to share, even with my brothers. Beast read the note quickly, his jaw tightening with each word.

"Two hundred grand by 6AM," he muttered, looking up at me. "Seven hours from now."

"Six hours and forty-three minutes," Hawk corrected, checking his watch. He pushed away from the wall and moved to look over Beast's shoulder at the note. "Amateurs?"

"Looks that way," I said, my voice flat. "Used a local kid as messenger. Couldn't even be bothered to type it up."

Beast nodded, eyes sharp as he assessed me. "The club has the money. We can have it ready in an hour."

I knew what he was doing -- laying out options, letting me know the full support of the Reckless Kings was behind me, whatever I decided. We'd never agreed to a ransom in the past, and I didn't want to start now. The leather of the worn couch creaked as I sank onto it, leaning forward with my elbows on my knees. My hands dangled between them, fingers laced together to hide their trembling.

"You've got eyes out?" I asked, already knowing the answer.

Hawk nodded. "Every brother not here is on the streets. Shield's got the Prospects taking turns monitoring cameras. We've got calls in to the Dixie Reapers and Devil's Boneyard for backup if we need it."

The mention of the allied clubs sent a surge of gratitude through me, momentarily cutting through the haze of rage and fear. This was what it meant to wear the patch -- to have brothers across the country ready to ride to your aid without question.

Beast tossed the note onto the table and moved to the small makeshift bar in the corner, something that hadn't been there just yesterday. The bottle clinked against glass as he poured three fingers of whiskey into each of three tumblers. He handed one to Hawk, another to me, keeping the third for himself.

"This is your call, brother," Beast said, his voice gruff but gentle. "Your family, your decision."

Hawk nodded, raising his glass slightly. "Whatever you need, we're behind you."

I stared into the amber liquid, seeing Yulia's eyes

reflected there. The defiance in them when she'd looked at the camera. The subtle message I'd read in her expression, in the tilt of her chin. *Do not pay. Do not follow their instructions. Come for us your way.*

The whiskey burned a trail down my throat as I downed it in one swallow, welcoming the heat that bloomed in my chest. I began to pace, boots heavy on the worn floor that had seen decades of similar deliberations. Life and death decisions. Business and blood.

"If we pay," I said finally, thinking out loud, "we tell these fuckers that the Reckless Kings can be extorted. That taking our families gets results." I shook my head, fury building behind my sternum. "And there's no guarantee they'll let Yulia and Clover go once they have the money."

Beast remained silent, watching me work through it. Hawk knocked back his whiskey and set the glass on the desk.

"Amateurs get nervous," Hawk said. "Make mistakes. Especially once they have what they want."

I nodded grimly. We all knew what that meant. Once the kidnappers had the money, Yulia and Clover became liabilities. Witnesses who could identify them.

"And if we don't pay," I continued, the muscle in my jaw jumping as I clenched my teeth, "we risk them hurting my family to prove they're serious."

"True," Beast acknowledged. "But paying doesn't eliminate that risk. It just changes the timing."

I stopped pacing, my hands curling into fists at my sides. The weight of the decision pressed down on me like a physical force. Behind the rage, behind the fear, I felt the crushing responsibility of choosing the path that would bring my family home safely.

Yulia's face flashed in my mind again -- not from

the kidnapper's photo, but from the fair earlier that day. The way she'd looked at me on the Ferris wheel, something warm and hopeful in her eyes. The almost-kiss by the roller coaster, Clover's interruption coming seconds before our lips would have met. The promise of later. A later that might never come if I made the wrong choice now.

"We're running out of time," Hawk said quietly, breaking into my thoughts.

I turned to face them both, decision crystallizing like ice in my veins. "I'm not giving those bastards a dime," I said, each word precise and final. "We find them, and we get my family back our way."

Beast nodded once, satisfaction gleaming in his eyes. "Your call, your lead. What's the first move?"

"Shield," I said immediately. "I need to know what he's found. Traffic cams, security footage, anything that might give us a direction." I pulled out my phone, checking the time. "Just a bit over six hours until their deadline. I want them found before then."

"And when we find them?" Hawk asked, though his tone made it clear he already knew the answer.

I met his gaze steadily, all hesitation gone. "When we find them, we show them exactly what happens when someone takes what belongs to a Reckless King."

Beast moved around the table, clapping a heavy hand on my shoulder. "The whole club rides with you on this, Salvation. Every brother, every resource. We don't stop until your family is home."

The solidarity should have comforted me, and on some level it did. But as I left Church and headed for the tech room, all I could think of was Yulia and Clover, bound and afraid in some unknown location. Of the men who'd dared to take them, who'd touched what was mine.

Those men were already dead. They just didn't know it yet.

* * *

Time was slipping by. I'd been in the tech room for over an hour. The place hummed with electronic life, the air noticeably cooler than the rest of the clubhouse to keep the equipment from overheating. Shield sat hunched before a bank of monitors, his fingers flying across the keyboard as streams of data reflected in his glasses. The blue glow from the screens cast everything in an eerie light, turning familiar faces into hollow-eyed ghosts. I stood behind him, too wired to sit, my eyes burning from staring at footage for what felt like an eternity, searching for any glimpse of the men who'd taken my family.

"Anything?" I asked, for perhaps the twentieth time in the last hour.

Shield didn't look away from his primary screen, where traffic camera footage from near the fairgrounds played at double speed. "Nothing definitive yet." His voice lacked its usual sardonic edge, replaced by the flat efficiency of a man who understood exactly what was at stake. "I've got algorithms scanning for any vehicles that left the fair parking lot within the timeframe, but the camera coverage is spotty at best."

I leaned forward, bracing my hands on the back of his chair. My shoulders ached with tension, every muscle in my body coiled tight. "Show me the footage from inside the fair again."

Shield nodded, pulling up a different window on one of the side monitors. Grainy security footage from the fairgrounds appeared -- a high angle shot of the midway where I'd last seen Yulia and Clover. I watched, breath caught in my throat, as tiny figures moved through the frame. There -- Clover stopping at a henna tattoo booth. I didn't see either me or Yulia, which meant she'd gone back without us. The moment of separation that had started this nightmare.

"Can you zoom in on that guy?" I pointed to a figure in a baseball cap hovering near the booth.

Shield manipulated the footage, enlarging the section I'd indicated, but the resolution degraded to near-uselessness. "Sorry. These security cams are shit quality. Can barely make out faces even at normal size."

I exhaled slowly through my nose, pushing down the frustration that threatened to boil over. "What about after? Any cameras catch them leaving?"

"Working on it." Shield switched screens, pulling up a patchwork of footage from different cameras around the fair's perimeter. "The problem is, I need something to work with -- a face, a vehicle, anything. Without that, it's like searching for a needle in a haystack."

I straightened, pacing behind his chair. The room was small, barely large enough for the equipment and the two of us. Hawk had joined us earlier but had left to coordinate the brothers searching the streets. Now it was just Shield, me, and the endless parade of faceless strangers on the monitors.

"What about traffic cams near the fairgrounds?" I asked. "Any vehicles leaving in a hurry? Or carrying too many passengers?"

"Running those now." Shield gestured to a monitor on his left where footage played at high speed. "I've got facial recognition scanning for Yulia and Clover in any vehicle leaving the area, but it's a slow process. And if they were forced to duck down..." He let the implication hang.

I resumed my pacing, three steps in one direction, three in the other. The minutes ticked by on the digital clock in the corner of the main screen. Each one taking us closer to the deadline. Closer to whatever these fuckers had planned if their demands weren't met.

"I've got every ATM camera, every store security system I can access," Shield continued, his voice a steady counterpoint to my restless movement. "Plus, I'm running the faces from that photo through recognition software, trying to ID our kidnappers. But they're not facing the camera directly, which complicates things."

In addition to the photo I had, they'd texted a few others. They'd probably been trying to scare me into complying, but these assholes weren't very smart. They'd managed to include themselves in the background.

The image of Yulia and Clover bound and captive seared through my mind again. I pulled it from my pocket, staring at their faces. At the determination in Yulia's eyes, the frightened defiance in Clover's. Something about that look…

"Wait." I moved back to Shield, placing the photo beside his keyboard. "Look at the wall behind them. The concrete."

Shield peered at it, then adjusted his glasses. "What am I looking for?"

"The pattern. It's not just plain concrete." I pointed to a faint line visible behind Yulia's shoulder. "That looks like a seam. And the texture -- it's not poured concrete. It's block."

Shield zoomed in on the section I'd indicated, enhancing the image despite its graininess. "You're right. Concrete block construction." He looked up at me. "That narrows things down, but not by much. Still thousands of buildings with that type of construction in the city."

"But it gives us something to work with." I felt the first flicker of hope since this nightmare began. "Industrial areas. Warehouses. Basements."

Shield nodded, already typing commands. "I'll cross-reference with property records, focus the search on areas with that type of construction." He glanced at the clock. "But it's still a massive area to cover before six in the morning."

I gripped the back of his chair, knuckles turning white. "They'll send instructions for the drop before then. When they do, we can trace the call, right?"

"If they call, yeah. But smart money says they'll use a burner phone, which complicates things." Shield didn't sugarcoat it. "And if they're cautious about the drop location…"

"These aren't professionals," I reminded him. "They're amateurs. They'll make mistakes."

"Let's hope so." Shield returned to his screens, cycling through more traffic footage. "I need something more specific, though. A license plate. A face clear enough to run through the system. Even the make and model of a vehicle would help narrow this down."

Hours passed like this -- Shield working methodically through footage, me alternating between watching over his shoulder and pacing the small room like a caged animal. Occasionally, a Prospect would bring in fresh coffee or an update from the brothers on the street. No sightings. No leads. Nothing solid to work with.

The digital clock showed roughly two hours until the deadline.

"Goddamnit!" I finally exploded, slamming my fist into the wall hard enough to dent the drywall. Pain shot up my arm, a welcome distraction from the helpless rage that had been building inside me. "We're running out of time!"

Shield didn't flinch at my outburst. Instead, he swiveled his chair to face me fully for the first time since we'd entered the room. "We'll find them, Salvation."

"When?" I demanded, my voice raw. "After these fuckers decide they're tired of waiting for money? After they decide Yulia and Clover are liabilities?"

"We're going to find them," Shield repeated, his normally detached demeanor giving way to quiet intensity. "I'm not stopping until we do. None of us are."

I leaned against the wall, suddenly exhausted. The fear, anger, and desperate hope pressed down on me. I looked at the photo again, at Yulia's face. At the woman who had become so much more than the scared girl I'd once rescued. At the daughter we'd raised together.

"I don't care how long it takes or what I have to do," I said, my voice dropping to a dangerous quiet. "I'm going to find them, and when I do, I'll make them wish they'd never touched my family."

Shield didn't offer empty reassurances. He simply nodded and turned back to his screens. "Then let's keep working."

I pushed away from the wall, forcing my focus back to the task at hand. Sometime in the last few hours, the chaotic mix of fear and rage in my chest had crystallized into something harder, more focused. A cold determination that burned like liquid nitrogen.

Yulia and Clover were out there, counting on me to find them. The clock was ticking. The kidnappers would make contact soon with instructions for the money drop -- money they would never receive. And when they did, when they revealed themselves in any way, I would be ready.

I settled into the chair beside Shield, gaze fixed on the screens as more footage scrolled past.

I would find my family. I would bring them home.

And heaven help anyone who stood in my way.

Chapter Six

Shield

My eyes burned from staring at screens for nearly twenty-four hours straight, first working on a project for Beast, then trying to locate Salvation's family. The blue glow of the screens made everything else in the tech room fade to shadows. I blinked hard, forcing my vision to refocus on the facial recognition software as it churned through another batch of potential matches. Time had become meaningless, marked only by empty coffee cups and the growing tightness in my shoulders. None of that mattered. Somewhere out there, Yulia and Clover were being held against their will, and every second I wasted was another second they remained in danger.

The digital clock in the corner of my main monitor flipped to 4:30 AM. Almost eight hours since they'd vanished from the fairgrounds.

I rolled my neck, vertebrae cracking in protest. The tech room had become my prison -- six monitors bathing me in their artificial light, walls covered with printouts of suspects and locations, the air thick with the smell of electronics and stale coffee. On the screens before me, the city revealed itself in fragments: traffic camera footage on one, intercepted text messages on another, potential hideout locations marked on a digital map on the third. The fourth ran facial recognition software, the fifth displayed known gang members from our database, and the sixth showed a live feed from the cameras around our compound.

My fingers flew across the keyboard, cross-referencing data points, chasing the ghost of a lead.

Most of the brothers were out searching the streets, following my digital breadcrumbs, while I remained here, eyes peeled for any mistake our targets might make.

"Come on, you bastards," I muttered, downing the last of my coffee. The liquid was cold and bitter, but it kept me upright. "Show me something."

The facial recognition software pinged, drawing my attention to the fourth monitor. A partial match on a possible suspect -- 63% confidence. Not great, but better than anything we'd had so far. I leaned forward, squinting at the grainy image captured from a gas station security camera three miles from the fairgrounds, timestamped just thirty minutes after Yulia and Clover disappeared.

The man's face was partially obscured by a baseball cap, but the program had matched the visible portion to a known member of the Southside Scorpions -- a small-time gang that had been trying to carve out territory on the edges of Reckless Kings' domain. I pulled up his file: Marcus "Snake" Devlin, arrested twice for assault, once for possession with intent to distribute. Not exactly kidnapping material, but desperate times made men do desperate things.

My pulse quickened as I followed the digital trail, tracking the vehicle -- a black panel van with tinted windows -- through a series of traffic cameras. The van headed east from the gas station, toward an industrial area where the Scorpions were known to operate. I overlaid the route onto our digital map, watching as it wound through the city before disappearing into a blind spot where camera coverage was spotty at best.

"Got you," I whispered, already reaching for my phone to alert the brothers. But something made me pause, a nagging doubt I couldn't ignore. I rewound the footage, watching it again at half speed. This time, I caught it -- a brief moment when the driver turned toward his side mirror, giving the camera a clear view of his profile.

It wasn't Snake. Similar build, similar cap, but definitely not him.

"Fuck!" I slammed my fist on the desk, sending an empty coffee cup rolling to the floor. Another dead end. Another wasted hour chasing shadows.

I leaned back in my chair, pressing the heels of my hands against my burning eyes. The exhaustion hit me in waves, tempting me to close my eyes, just for a moment. But every time I did, I saw Clover's face -- so much like her mother's, always ready with a smart remark or quick smile. And Yulia, who'd overcome so much, who'd built a life from the ashes of her past. Who might finally have found happiness with Salvation if given the chance.

No. Sleep wasn't an option. Not until they were home.

I grabbed the last cold cup of coffee from the desk, grimacing as I swallowed the sludge. The caffeine barely registered anymore, but the ritual itself helped clear my head. I returned to the screens, methodically reviewing what we knew so far.

The kidnappers were amateurs -- that much was clear from their sloppy ransom demand and use of a child messenger. They'd taken Yulia and Clover from the fairgrounds without raising alarms, suggesting they'd planned it in advance. They knew enough about the club to target Salvation's family specifically. And they were confident enough to set a ransom deadline.

But who were they? What did they really want? And most importantly, where were they keeping Yulia and Clover?

I pulled up the photo that had accompanied the ransom note, the one showing Yulia and Clover bound against a concrete wall. We'd analyzed every pixel of that image, trying to extract clues from the background. Concrete block construction, poor lighting, no windows visible. It narrowed things down to industrial buildings, warehouses, or basements, but that still left hundreds of potential locations across the city.

The door to the tech room creaked open behind me. I didn't need to turn around to know who it was -- Salvation's heavy footsteps were unmistakable, as was the weight of his presence. He'd been prowling the compound like a caged predator, alternating between the tech room and the war room, unable to settle anywhere while his family remained missing.

"Anything?" His voice was a rough whisper, stripped raw by worry and rage.

I swiveled my chair to face him, taking in his haggard appearance. His knuckles were raw -- from punching walls, most likely. The calm, controlled Salvation I'd known for years had been replaced by something feral, dangerous.

"I might have something," I said, gesturing him closer. No point mentioning the false lead with the Scorpions -- he needed hope, not more disappointment. "Not a location yet, but patterns. Come look."

He moved to stand behind me, his breathing too controlled, too measured -- a man holding himself together through sheer force of will.

"I've been tracking cell tower activity near the fairgrounds around the time of the abduction," I explained, pulling up a new set of data on the center screen. "There's a spike in activity that doesn't match normal patterns. Someone was making a lot of calls in a short period."

"Can you trace the numbers?"

"Burners, most likely. But I've cross-referenced with known associates of every gang and crew in the area." I pointed to a cluster of dots on the digital map. "These calls pinged off towers in this ten-block radius. And three of the numbers have connections to the same group of low-level dealers who operate out of the Westridge neighborhood."

It wasn't much. Barely even a lead. But it was all I had after hours of searching.

Salvation's hand gripped my shoulder, his fingers digging in painfully. "Show me."

* * *

Salvation

I marked another X on the map with savage precision, the red marker squeaking against laminated paper. Another dead end. Another location cleared. Another hour gone with Yulia and Clover still missing. The war room had become my personal hell -- a space where hope flickered and died with each incoming call, each crossed-out location, each fading lead. I resumed pacing, my boots echoing on the wooden floor as I circled the large table for what felt like the thousandth time, as if movement alone could somehow conjure the answers that continued to elude us.

Photos of known gang territories, printouts of Shield's technical data, lists of abandoned properties that matched the concrete construction we'd identified from the ransom photo. Red Xs marred most of them now -- warehouses cleared, safehouses raided, leads exhausted. My brothers had torn through the city like a hurricane, leaving terrified informants and smashed doors in their wake, all with nothing to show for it.

In the center of the corkboard hung the photo I couldn't stop staring at -- Yulia and Clover at the fairgrounds, taken not long before they disappeared. I'd snapped it without them noticing, capturing a moment of happiness I'd taken for granted.

My phone vibrated against my hip. I snatched it up, pressing it to my ear without checking the caller ID.

"Tell me something good," I demanded, my voice raw from lack of sleep.

"Nothing at the Southside warehouses." Beast's deep voice rumbled through the connection, exhaustion evident even through the static. "We've cleared every building on our list, turned over every rock. No sign of them."

I closed my eyes, swallowing the bitter taste of disappointment. "What about the Scorpions' clubhouse? I overheard Shield mentioning it to Ranger."

"Empty. Looks like they cleared out in a hurry, but not recently. Place was already covered in dust."

My free hand clenched into a fist, knuckles still raw from earlier connections with walls that couldn't fight back. "Keep looking. There has to be something we're missing."

"We will." A pause, then Beast's voice softened slightly. "How're you holding up, brother?"

"I'll hold up when they're home," I answered, ending the call before he could respond.

Yulia and Clover had been gone for too many hours. The 6 AM deadline had come and passed with no word from the kidnappers. Shield's theory was that they were waiting us out, thinking the silence would make us desperate enough to pay on any terms. He was probably right, but knowing their strategy didn't bring us any closer to finding them.

I studied the map again, tracing the routes we'd already searched, the buildings we'd already cleared. My vision blurred momentarily, fatigue and worry creating a haze I forced myself to blink away. I couldn't afford weakness now. Not when Yulia and Clover were counting on me.

Yulia. The last time I'd seen her, we'd been so close to crossing the line we'd danced around for too long. Her gaze had met mine with such warmth, such promise. And Clover, my daughter in every way that mattered, her future stretching bright and limitless before her. Both of them, taken from me in an instant because I'd let my guard down. Because I'd forgotten, just for one day, the constant vigilance that kept our world safe.

My phone vibrated again. Hawk this time.

"Downtown's clear," he reported without preamble. "We've hit every location on Shield's list. Nothing."

"What about the building on Parkway? The one with the loading docks?"

"First place we checked. No one's been there in months."

I pressed my fingers against my closed eyes, the pressure doing nothing to relieve the throbbing headache building behind them. "What about informants? Someone has to know something."

"Everyone's scared silent or genuinely clueless." Hawk's frustration matched my own. "We've twisted every arm, called in every favor. It's like they vanished into thin air."

But they hadn't. They were somewhere in this

city, being held by men who'd been bold enough to take them but hadn't been heard from since missing their own deadline. What did that mean? Were they having second thoughts? Changing plans? Or…

I shut down that line of thinking before it could fully form. I couldn't afford to consider the worst-case scenarios. Not yet.

"Keep pushing," I told Hawk. "These guys aren't professionals. They'll surface eventually."

After disconnecting, I braced both hands against the table, letting my head hang for just a moment. Exhaustion pulled at me like quicksand, threatening to drag me under. I'd been running on rage and fear for hours, and both were starting to wear thin, leaving only a bone-deep weariness in their wake.

My gaze fell on the photo again. I reached out with unsteady fingers, tracing Yulia's face through the glossy paper. Her eyes, so blue they seemed to pierce right through you. The slight curve of her lips that had taken years to appear after I'd first brought her to the compound, a frightened girl with scars on her wrists and emptiness in her gaze.

Eleven years we'd been married. All those years, I'd kept my distance, telling myself it was for her sake. That she needed security, not complications. That friendship was enough.

What a fucking waste.

My jaw clenched as I stared at her face in the photo, the weight of unspoken words sitting heavy in my chest. If -- when -- I got her back, I wouldn't waste another day. Another moment.

A sound escaped me, something between a growl and a sigh. I pushed away from the table, resuming my pacing. The floor creaked beneath my boots, the sound oddly comforting in the too-quiet room. Outside, the compound was eerily empty, most of our brothers still combing the city. Those who remained moved with purpose, gathering information, coordinating search parties, following whatever leads Shield found.

I paused at the window, staring out at the early rays of sunlight. Somewhere out there, Yulia and Clover were waiting. Counting on me to find them. To bring them home.

"I'm coming," I whispered, the promise fogging the glass briefly before fading away. "Hold on just a little longer."

I turned back to the war room, to the maps and photos and fading hopes. Sleep wasn't an option. Rest wasn't an option. Not until my family was safe.

The door to the war room creaked open, breaking my dark thoughts. Prospero stood in the doorway, two steaming cups of coffee in his hands, his expression calm despite the chaos that had engulfed the club. The treasurer had always been the steady one -- analytical, composed, a counterbalance to the more volatile temperaments that filled our ranks. Right now, that steadiness felt like both a blessing and an irritation, highlighting my own fraying control.

"Thought you could use this," he said, crossing the room to set one cup on the table near me. "It's the good stuff, not that sludge from the main pot."

I nodded my thanks, wrapping my fingers around the warm mug. Prospero didn't speak immediately, giving me space as he surveyed the room, taking in the maps, the photos, the growing evidence of my desperation.

"Any word?" he finally asked, his voice carefully neutral.

"Nothing new." The coffee scalded my throat as I

swallowed. "Shield's working an angle with some cell data. Beast and Hawk are still out searching. But we're just…" I gestured at the map, the red Xs mocking me. "We're going in circles."

Prospero leaned against the edge of the table, studying me over the rim of his mug. Unlike most of us, he looked relatively put-together despite the crisis -- his blond hair combed, his clothes unwrinkled. Only the shadows under his blue eyes betrayed his own exhaustion.

"You should get some rest," he said. "Even an hour would help. You're no good to them running on fumes."

"I can't." The words came out sharper than intended. "Every time I close my eyes, I see them. Bound. Afraid. Wondering why the hell I haven't found them yet."

Prospero didn't flinch at my tone. "They're strong, both of them. Yulia especially. She's survived worse."

"That's the fucking point," I said, setting the mug down so hard coffee sloshed over the rim. "She's been through enough. She deserves better than this. Better than --" I cut myself off, turning to stare at the wall of information that had yielded nothing useful.

"Better than what?" Prospero pressed gently.

I pressed my palms against my eyes, the pressure building behind them threatening to erupt in a way I couldn't afford. When I lowered my hands, my gaze caught on the photo of Yulia and Clover again.

"I fucked up," I admitted, my voice rough with emotion. "I had years to tell her how I felt, and now…" I shook my head, unable to finish the thought.

Understanding dawned in Prospero's eyes. Unlike some of the newer brothers, he'd known the full story from the beginning -- how I'd married Yulia to protect her from her father's enemies, how our arrangement had been on paper only. He'd been there when I'd brought her home, a terrified girl who flinched at sudden movements and couldn't sleep without a light on. He'd watched as she slowly rebuilt herself, as our relationship evolved from protector and protected to something more complex, more meaningful.

"You'll get the chance to tell her," he said with quiet certainty. "We'll do whatever it takes to get your wife and daughter back."

"It shouldn't have taken this." I gestured around the room, at the evidence of our desperate search. "Eleven years. Eleven fucking years of living under the same roof, raising Clover together, and I never had the balls to just say it. To tell her that somewhere along the line, that marriage license became real for me."

Prospero set his coffee down and stepped closer, placing a firm hand on my shoulder. "You were respecting her boundaries. After what she'd been through, you didn't want to pressure her."

"Maybe at first," I conceded. "But these last few years? That was just cowardice. Fear that she'd reject me. That I'd lose what we had." A bitter laugh escaped me. "And now I might lose her anyway."

"That's not going to happen." Prospero's grip on my shoulder tightened. "Listen to me, Salvation. We will find them and bring them home. And then you can spend the next fifty years making up for lost time."

Something about his certainty, the absolute conviction in his voice, eased the vise around my chest just slightly. This was why Prospero was our treasurer, our voice of reason. When he spoke with that tone, you believed him, no matter how dire the circumstances.

Before I could respond, the shrill ring of the club phone cut through the room like a physical presence. We both froze, eyes locked on the ancient landline that sat on a side table -- the dedicated line we never disconnected, the number known only to club members and a select few allies.

My heart slammed against my ribs as I crossed to it in two strides. Prospero was already moving, grabbing a pen and pad of paper from the desk.

"Put it on speaker," he said. "Might be able to hear something in the background."

I nodded, lifting the handset and pressing the speaker button in one motion. "Talk," I demanded, my voice controlled despite the adrenaline surging through me.

"Reckless Kings." The voice was digitally distorted, unrecognizable. "You missed our deadline."

"*You* missed it," I countered, my knuckles white around the handset. "Hard to deliver money when you don't provide instructions."

A mechanized laugh grated through the speaker. "Just testing your resolve. Seeing how serious you are about getting your family back."

Prospero pointed to his watch, mouthing "Keep him talking" as he scribbled something on the pad and walked out. Tracing the call, most likely, though we both knew it was probably a burner.

"I'm dead serious," I said, emphasizing each word. "But I need proof they're alive and unharmed. Now."

"They're fine. For now." The distorted voice paused, and I heard muffled sounds in the background, like someone moving around. "But that could change if you keep stalling. Two hundred thousand."

"I want to talk to them first."

Another pause, longer this time. "Not happening. You're not in a position to make demands."

My free hand curled into a fist, nails digging crescents into my palm. "Then how do I know they're alive?"

"Fair point." The voice seemed to consider this. "I'll send you a photo. One time offer. Then you deliver the money, and this ends happily for everyone."

"When and where?" I asked, struggling to keep my voice level. Prospero came back into the room but didn't say anything. I hoped he'd given the information to Shield and we'd have a location from this phone call.

"We haven't seen any movement on your end to gather the cash, which means you'll need more time. You have forty-eight hours. I'll text instructions to your number." A pause. "Don't try anything stupid. We're watching. And we're not alone."

"If you hurt them," I said, each word precisely enunciated, "there won't be a hole deep enough for you to hide in. I will find you. And I *will* end you."

The digitized laugh came again, sending ice through my veins. "Big talk from a man who can't even find his own family. Forty-eight hours. Be ready."

The line went dead.

For a moment, neither of us moved. The silence in the room felt oppressive, broken only by our breathing.

"They're still alive," he said finally, his tone cautiously optimistic. "And we've got more time."

I replaced the handset with deliberate care, fighting the urge to rip the entire phone from the wall.

"What did you get?"

Prospero slid the pad toward me. "Background noise suggests some kind of mechanical system. Maybe a furnace or generator. And I caught what sounded like a train whistle, very faint. I asked Shield to trace them, but the call probably ended too soon."

I stared at his notes, mind racing. "Industrial area near the train tracks."

"Narrows it down." Prospero nodded. "And the new deadline gives Shield more time to trace the photo when it comes in."

I straightened, a cold clarity replacing the fog of exhaustion and despair that had clouded my thoughts. Two days. We had two days to find them before the kidnappers expected their money.

"Get Shield," I said, already moving toward the door. "Tell Beast and Hawk to regroup. We need everyone back here within the hour."

"Where are you going?" Prospero called after me.

I paused at the threshold, my hand on the doorframe. "To wake up every informant, snitch, and lowlife who might know something about abandoned buildings near the train tracks." I glanced back at him. "We've got forty-eight hours to turn this city upside down. And that's exactly what we're going to do."

Chapter Seven

Salvation

I stood in the doorway of the war room, watching as Beast spread a detailed map across the worn wooden table. The fluorescent lights cast harsh shadows across his face, deepening the lines of exhaustion and determination etched there. Around him, my brothers gathered, their expressions grim as they took in the layout of the industrial district where our family was being held. Hours of rage had been building in my chest, hardening into something cold and lethal. Now, finally, we had a location. And a plan.

"Here's the drop point." Beast's finger jabbed at a spot on the map -- a closed gas station about two blocks from an abandoned warehouse near the rail yard. "Shield triangulated the cell tower pings and confirmed it with satellite imagery. High probability they're holding Yulia and Clover inside that warehouse."

I moved closer, scanning the blueprint that Shield had somehow acquired and printed out. The warehouse was two stories, with multiple entry points and a large loading dock facing away from the main road. Perfect for moving things -- or people -- without being noticed.

"We go in here, here, and here," Beast continued, marking three entry points with a red marker. His movements were precise, calculated -- the strategist I'd trusted with my life for over a decade. "Drifter, you and Patriot take position in these unmarked vehicles. Set up surveillance two hours before the drop time. I want eyes on every approach."

Drifter nodded, his usually relaxed demeanor replaced by focused intensity. "We'll see them coming."

"The rest of us prepare for extraction," Beast said, looking around the table at each brother in turn. "We'll have three teams. Assault, perimeter security, and extraction. Once we confirm Yulia and Clover are inside, we move fast and clean."

My knuckles turned white as I gripped the edge of the table, leaning forward to study the building's layout. "I'm leading the assault team."

The room went silent. Beast's eyes met mine across the table, concern evident in his gaze. "Salvation, I think --"

"This is my family," I cut him off, my voice low and dangerous. "My wife. My daughter. I'm going in first."

The words hung in the air between us. My wife. Not just on paper anymore. Not just a legal arrangement for protection. For the first time, I'd said it out loud, claimed her in front of my brothers without qualification or explanation. No one reacted. It made me wonder if they'd figured it out long before I'd even admitted it to myself.

He studied me for a long moment, measuring my control against my rage. Finally, he nodded once. "You lead the assault team. But you follow the plan. No cowboy shit. No lone wolf heroics. Clear?"

"Crystal." I forced my fingers to release their death grip on the table edge.

"Hawk, you and Cyclops flank Salvation," Beast continued, getting back to business. "Nitro, Friar, and I will be right behind you. Second team takes the perimeter -- Prospero, you coordinate that with the Prospects. No one gets in or out once we're engaged."

Prospero nodded, already pulling a smaller map toward him to mark positions.

"What about the ransom?" Hawk asked, voicing the question hanging over all of us. "Just in case, I made sure two hundred K was ready, but if we're going in hot…"

"Decoy package," Beast answered. "We make the drop as instructed, buy ourselves time to get into position while they're distracted. By the time they realize it's filled with newspaper, we'll already be inside."

I nodded my approval. Smart. Keep them focused on the money while we closed the trap around them. Although, that also assumed they would actually take the bait.

The war room door opened, and Dr. Kestral poked his head in. I stepped out to follow him, thinking he must need something. The club doctor -- Prospero's brother by blood -- moved to the newly added infirmary and began checking supplies and packing a medical bag.

"Any word on their condition?" he asked, his voice calm and professional as he began unpacking supplies with methodical precision.

"Unknown," Beast replied. I glanced over my shoulder, not realizing he'd even followed us. "Last visual confirmation was the photo they sent, showing them bound but apparently unharmed."

I watched as Dr. Kestral laid out gauze, antiseptic, suture kits, and more specialized equipment I couldn't name. His movements were practiced and efficient, a man preparing for the worst while hoping for the best. He checked each item twice, then reopened his emergency kit to verify its contents for a third time.

"I'll be ready," he said simply, glancing my way with quiet reassurance.

The planning continued, each detail meticulously covered. Escape routes. Communication protocols. Contingencies for every scenario we could imagine. Throughout it all, I felt a strange calm settling over me -- not peace, but the focused clarity that comes before violence. The rage hadn't disappeared. It had transformed, becoming something I could direct with precision.

"We move out ninety minutes from now," Beast concluded. "Gear up."

The brothers dispersed to prepare, the room emptying until only Beast and I remained. He rolled up the map, his movements deliberate.

"You good?" he asked quietly.

"I will be when they're home."

He clasped my shoulder, squeezing once. "We'll get them back."

I nodded, unable to form words around the knot in my throat. Then I headed to the armory, where my brothers were already selecting their weapons. It was one of the many changes this place had undergone over the past decade.

The room hummed with focused energy as hands checked magazines, tested knife edges, and adjusted tactical gear. No jokes, no banter -- just the quiet efficiency of men preparing for war. I strapped my Glock to my thigh, checked the action on my backup piece, and slid a hunting knife into my boot. The weight of the weapons was comforting, grounding.

Hawk approached, handing me a tactical vest. "Shield got thermal imaging of the building. Heat signatures suggest at least six tangos inside, plus two smaller signatures that match Yulia and Clover's profiles. Second floor, northeast corner. Looks like they've moved them."

I nodded, memorizing the location. Six against twelve. Good odds, especially with surprise on our side.

"You ready for this?" Hawk asked, his voice low enough that only I could hear.

"Been ready," I replied, checking the extra magazines on my belt.

He studied my face for a moment. "Just remember -- mission first. Getting them out safely is what matters. Everything else is secondary."

I knew what he was saying. Don't lose yourself to revenge. Don't put payback before rescue. I wanted to promise him I'd keep my focus, but I couldn't lie to my brother.

"I'm going to kill every last one of them," I said instead, my voice flat and certain.

Hawk didn't argue. He just nodded once and moved away to finish his own preparations.

As the minutes ticked down toward departure, I found myself standing before the wall of photos in the main room of the clubhouse. My eyes fixed on one particular image -- Yulia, Clover, and me at Clover's sixteenth birthday earlier that year. We were smiling, Clover in the center with birthday cake frosting on her nose, Yulia and I on either side of her. A family portrait in everything but name.

I touched the photo briefly, a promise without words. Then I turned and walked out to the line of bikes waiting in the compound, the weight of guns and knives nothing compared to the weight of responsibility pressing down on my shoulders.

The sun was rising into the sky as we mounted

up. No colors -- just black leather and deadly purpose. Beast gave the signal, and engines roared to life in unison.

It was time to bring my family home.

* * *

We approached the concrete block building like shadows. No engine noise for the final quarter mile. Hawk, Cyclops, and I led the way, our boots silent on the cracked pavement as we closed in on the warehouse. I felt the weight of my Glock against my thigh, the knife at my ankle, tools that would soon be slick with blood. Somewhere inside that building, behind those weathered walls, Yulia and Clover waited. My family. The thought sharpened my focus to a razor's edge, the world narrowing to this moment, this mission, this kill.

"Three heat signatures on the first floor," Shield murmured into our earpieces, his voice flat and technical from his position in the surveillance van. "Two near the front entrance, one patrolling the east corridor. Upper floor shows four more, plus the two smaller signatures in the northeast corner."

I caught Hawk's eye, a silent confirmation passing between us. Yulia and Clover were still here. Still alive. The relief that flooded through me lasted only a second before hardening back into deadly purpose.

"Confirm positions," Beast's voice came through the comm.

"Perimeter team in position," Prospero responded. "All exit points covered."

"Surveillance is go," Drifter added. "Street's clear. No movement."

I pulled my Glock from its holster, screwing the silencer onto the barrel with practiced fingers. Around me, my brothers did the same, their movements fluid and precise in the gathering darkness.

"On my mark," Beast said, his voice steady as a heartbeat. "Three, two, one. Execute."

We moved as one, splitting into our assigned teams. Hawk, Cyclops, and I approached the side entrance while Beast led his group toward the loading dock. The third team circled to the rear fire exit. The building loomed before us, its windows dark and empty, like eye sockets in a skull.

Cyclops reached the door first, testing the handle. Locked. He pulled a set of picks from his cut and went to work, his good eye focused intensely on the task. Ten seconds later, I heard a soft *click*. He nodded once, tucking the picks away.

I took position, weapon raised. Hawk and Cyclops flanked me, their breathing as controlled as my own. With my free hand, I gripped the door handle, then pulled it open.

The hallway beyond was dim, lit only by emergency exit signs that cast a sickly red glow over peeling paint and concrete floors. The scent of mildew and cigarettes hit me as we slipped inside, the door closing silently behind us. For a moment, we froze, listening.

Footsteps approached from around the corner. Slow, casual. A guard making his rounds. I pressed my back against the wall, signaling to Hawk and Cyclops to hold position. The footsteps grew louder, accompanied by the soft crackle of a radio.

"Perimeter check. All clear," a male voice reported into the radio. "Next check in thirty."

The guard rounded the corner, a pistol held loosely at his side, completely unaware of what waited for him. I moved before he could register our presence, my hand clamping over his mouth as I slammed his head into the concrete wall with enough force to daze him. His radio clattered to the floor as Cyclops caught his weapon arm, twisting until something snapped. The man tried to scream, the sound muffled against my palm.

"Where are they?" I hissed into his ear, easing the pressure on his mouth just enough to allow an answer.

His eyes, wide with terror, darted toward the ceiling. "Upstairs," he gasped. "End of the hall. Please -
-"

I cut off his plea by slamming his head into the wall again, harder this time. His body went limp. I lowered him to the ground as Hawk retrieved the fallen radio, silencing it before any alarm could be raised.

"One down," I murmured into my comm. "Moving to the stairwell."

"Copy," Beast responded. "We've cleared the loading dock. Two tangos neutralized. Moving to join you."

We advanced through the corridor, weapons ready, each of us scanning different angles. The building was older than it had appeared from outside, the interior a maze of narrow hallways and storage rooms. Most doors stood open, revealing empty spaces filled with dust and forgotten debris. This place had been abandoned long before the kidnappers chose it as their hideout.

The stairwell door appeared ahead, marked by a faded exit sign. Hawk moved forward, checking the push bar for any wires or triggers. Finding none, he eased it open just enough to peer through.

"Clear," he whispered. "Stairs go up to the

second level. I hear voices."

I took point, leading the way into the stairwell. Our boots made no sound on the concrete steps as we ascended, the silence broken only by our measured breathing and the soft creak of leather. At the top landing, I paused, ear pressed against the metal door.

"-- time's running out," a voice said from the other side. "They've had long enough. If they don't make the drop in the next hour --"

"They'll pay," another voice interrupted. "They've got no choice. Not if they want the girl and the Russian back in one piece."

My fingers tightened around the grip of my Glock, rage flaring hot and bright in my chest. The Russian. Yulia. My wife. These men had dared to take her, to threaten her. Had dared to put their hands on my daughter. The urge to burst through the door, to end them all in a hail of bullets, was nearly overwhelming.

Hawk's hand on my shoulder brought me back, a silent reminder of the plan. Get to Yulia and Clover first. Everything else was secondary.

"Beast's team is in position at the east stairwell." Shield's voice came through the comm. "Three more heat signatures on your floor, plus two smaller ones and one of an average-size male in another area, directly ahead and to the right of your position."

I took a deep breath, steadying myself. "Copy. Moving in."

Cyclops took position beside me, his hand on the door handle. I nodded once, and he pulled it open just enough for us to slip through one by one.

The second floor was divided into what had once been offices, most walls now crumbling, doors hanging from broken hinges. Two men stood at the far end of the corridor, smoking cigarettes, their backs to us. A third sat in a folding chair outside what appeared to be an intact room, a shotgun balanced across his knees.

We moved silently, using the shadows and debris for cover. I signaled to Hawk to take the two smokers while Cyclops and I approached the guard with the shotgun. My heart hammered against my ribs, but my hands remained steady, my mind clear and cold as ice.

The guard never saw us coming. Cyclops moved first, a blur of controlled violence as he wrenched the shotgun away and drove his knife deep into the man's thigh, severing the femoral artery. I clamped my hand over his mouth, muffling his scream as his life pumped out in rhythmic spurts. His eyes bulged with shock and pain, locking with mine for one terrible moment before glazing over.

At the end of the corridor, Hawk took down the two smokers with brutal efficiency -- a silenced shot to the back of the head for one, his knife across the throat of the other. Neither had time to raise an alarm.

"Clear," Hawk whispered, already moving to join us.

The door the guard had been watching was reinforced, a new deadbolt installed in the old frame. Behind it, I could hear muffled voices. One of them -- a soft, accented murmur -- sent a jolt of recognition through me. Yulia.

My breathing became ragged, the control I'd maintained since entering the building beginning to slip. So close. They were just on the other side of this door. I tried the handle. Locked, as expected.

"Stand back," I growled, no longer caring about stealth. I aimed my Glock at the lock and fired twice, the silencer reducing the shots to dull thuds.

The voices inside went silent. Then came a man's shout, followed by Clover's muffled cry. The sound of my daughter in distress shattered the last of my restraint.

I kicked the door with everything I had, wood splintering around the lock as it burst open. The scene inside burned into my brain like acid -- Yulia and Clover bound to metal chairs in the center of a bare concrete room, zip ties cutting into their wrists and ankles. Yulia's face was bruised along one cheekbone, Clover's eyes red from crying. But what sent white-hot rage exploding through my veins was the man standing between them, a hunting knife held casually against Clover's cheek. He spun toward the doorway as I entered, his face twisting into a sneer beneath a snake tattoo that curled up his neck.

"Well, well," he drawled, pressing the blade closer to Clover's skin. "Looks like daddy didn't pay up after all." He shifted his weight, positioning himself behind Clover's chair, using her as a shield. "That's disappointing. Time to send a message about what happens when you don't follow instructions."

Clover whimpered as a thin line of blood appeared on her cheek. Yulia strained against her bonds, her blue eyes locking with mine across the room -- not in fear, but in absolute certainty. Even now, after everything, she believed in me completely. That trust hit me harder than any bullet ever could.

"You're already dead," I said, my voice unnaturally calm despite the storm raging inside me. "You just don't know it yet."

The man laughed, the sound as ugly as the tattoo on his neck. "Big talk from someone whose kid is about to lose an eye." He adjusted his grip on the knife. "Drop your weapon or the girl gets it first. Then I'll take my time with the Russian."

Behind me, I sensed Hawk and Cyclops entering the room, spreading out to cover the angles. The kidnapper's eyes darted between us, the first flicker of uncertainty crossing his face as he realized he was outnumbered.

I lowered my gun slowly, placing it on the floor. "Let them go," I said, raising my empty hands. "This is between you and me now."

"That's right," he said, his confidence returning. "Nice and easy. Now kick it over here."

I complied, sending the Glock sliding across the concrete floor away from both of us. The man's eyes followed it for a split second -- his first and final mistake.

I lunged forward with a roar that didn't sound human even to my own ears, covering the distance between us in two strides. The knife slashed out, missing my face by inches as I ducked under his swing and tackled him away from Clover's chair. We crashed to the floor, his head cracking against the concrete with a satisfying *thud.*

He was strong, most likely muscled from prison workouts and street fights. The knife flashed again, slicing through my sleeve and into the meat of my forearm. I barely felt it. All I could see was Yulia's bruised face, Clover's bleeding cheek. All I could think was, *Mine. He hurt what's mine.*

My fist connected with his jaw, snapping his head back. Again. Again. Blood sprayed from his split lips, speckling my face, my hands. He tried to stab me, his movements becoming desperate as I rained blows down on him. I caught his wrist mid-thrust, twisting with all my strength until the bones gave way with a wet *snap.*

He screamed, the knife clattering to the ground. I grabbed it before he could recover, the handle slick with both our blood now. His eyes widened as he realized what was coming.

"Wait," he gasped, "I can tell you --"

I drove the blade into his stomach, cutting off whatever lie he'd been about to offer. His body arched in shock and pain as I pulled the knife out, only to plunge it in again. And again. Blood bubbled from his mouth, his eyes wide with disbelief.

"This is for my wife," I growled, twisting the blade deeper. "And this --" I yanked it free, blood spraying across the concrete, "-- is for my daughter." In one fluid motion, I drew the knife across his throat, opening him from ear to ear. He made a wet, gurgling sound as his lifeblood pumped onto the floor beneath him, his eyes fixed on mine until the light in them flickered and died.

Only then did I become aware of someone calling my name. Hawk stood over me, his expression grim. "Salvation," he said, his voice breaking through the red haze of my rage. "It's done. He's gone. Your family needs you now."

I staggered to my feet, suddenly conscious of the blood covering my hands, my arms, soaking into my clothes. Yulia and Clover were watching me, their eyes wide. For a terrible moment, I wondered if I'd frightened them -- if they'd look at me differently now that they'd seen what I was capable of.

Cyclops was already cutting through Clover's zip ties with a tactical knife, his movements quick but gentle. I moved to Yulia, the dead man's knife still clutched in my hand. When I realized what I was holding, I dropped it as if it had burned me, wiping my bloody hands on my jeans before yanking my own knife free and reaching for her bonds. "Are you hurt?" I asked, my voice rough with emotion as I worked on the zip ties around her wrists. "Did they --"

"We're okay," she said, her accent thicker than usual with stress and exhaustion. "Nothing that won't heal."

There was so much I wanted to say, to ask, but I held back. It could wait. Right now, I needed to make sure they hadn't been hurt too badly and get them home. Which meant taking a step back and letting the doctor do his job.

Chapter Eight

Salvation

Blood covered my hands. Most of it was his. The man who'd dared to hurt my family. I knelt on the concrete floor beside Yulia and Clover, their bound wrists now free but marked with angry red welts from the zip ties. The room stank of violence -- copper-tang of blood, acrid sweat of fear. But all I could focus on was my family. Alive. Breathing. Safe.

"Don't move yet," Dr. Kestral said, shouldering his way past Hawk to kneel beside us. The medical bag he carried looked out of place among the broken furniture and blood-spattered concrete. His hands were steady as he opened it, the movements precise and practiced. "Let me check them over first."

I shifted back to give him room, my gaze never leaving Yulia and Clover. The doctor's face gave nothing away as he gently tilted Yulia's chin, examining the bruise blooming across her cheek. His fingers probed with clinical detachment, but I flinched with each touch as if feeling the pain myself. I didn't ask, but I had a feeling he was making sure nothing was broken.

"Superficial," he murmured, reaching for a penlight to check her pupils. "Any dizziness? Nausea?"

Yulia shook her head slightly. "No. Just tired."

"And thirsty," Clover added, her voice small and scratchy. "They didn't give us much water."

The words hit me like physical blows. Each detail of their suffering carved new wounds into me. I should have found them sooner. Should have prevented this entirely. My hands clenched into fists, dried blood cracking across my knuckles.

Dr. Kestral turned his attention to Yulia's wrists, where the zip ties had bitten deep enough to break skin in places. He cleaned each abrasion with antiseptic wipes, the sharp medicinal smell cutting through the heavier scents of blood and fear.

"Any other injuries I should know about?" he asked, his tone remaining professional, detached.

Yulia hesitated, then lifted the edge of her shirt slightly to reveal a mottled bruise across her ribs. "One of them kicked me. When I tried to keep them away from Clover."

My vision went red around the edges. I'd killed the man with the snake tattoo, but there had been others. Others who'd put their hands on my wife, who'd hurt her while I spent hours searching in the wrong places. Others who still deserved to die. I still didn't know for sure if they were related to the Scorpions, and I'd leave that detail to the others. None of it mattered. As long as they were dead, I was satisfied.

"Likely bruised ribs, not broken," Dr. Kestral said after a careful examination. "Deep breaths hurt?"

"Yes."

"We'll wrap them at the compound. Nothing's displaced." He applied some kind of cream to her wrists before wrapping them in loose gauze. "This will help with the pain and prevent infection until we can get you cleaned up. I'll re-treat them once we're at the compound."

Throughout it all, Yulia's gaze kept finding mine, as if reassuring herself I was really there. The trust I saw there felt like fire against my skin. I didn't deserve it. Not when I'd failed to protect her in the first place.

Dr. Kestral shifted to Clover, his hands even gentler as he examined the cut on her cheek. The thin line of blood had dried, stark against her pale skin. She tried not to wince as he cleaned it, but I caught the small, pained breath she took.

"Won't need stitches," he said, reaching for a butterfly bandage. "But it might leave a small scar."

A scar. On my daughter's face. Because I hadn't been there to stop it. Now she'd have that on top of the burn scars on the other side.

"It's okay, Dad," Clover said, reading my expression with uncanny accuracy. "I'm okay."

Her voice cracked on the last word, the brave facade finally slipping. Tears welled in her eyes, the first she'd allowed herself since we'd burst through the door. My arm moved automatically to comfort her, reaching out before I remembered the dried blood still coating my hands and forearms. I froze, suddenly conscious of what I must look like to them -- covered in another man's blood, hands that had just taken a life with brutal efficiency. I pulled back, not wanting to soil them further, to mark them with the evidence of what I'd done.

Clover's eyes followed the movement, understanding dawning in her tear-filled gaze. "Dad?"

"You're safe now," I managed, my voice rougher than I intended. "That's all that matters."

Dr. Kestral finished placing the bandage on her cheek, then checked her wrists as he had Yulia's. More abrasions, more evidence of their ordeal. Each injury he treated felt like an accusation -- *you weren't there, you were too late, you failed them.*

"Dehydrated, exhausted, some minor injuries," he concluded. "Let me take a look at you." Ignoring my attempt to wave him off, he bandaged my arm, then began packing his supplies back into his bag. "Nothing life-threatening for any of you, but they need rest, fluids, and monitoring for the next twenty-four hours."

I nodded, unable to form words past the tightness in my throat. The doctor stood, moving back to give us space, but I remained where I was, paralyzed by the blood drying on my skin. It flaked when I flexed my fingers, falling to the concrete like rust.

Yulia's eyes never left my face. "I never had any doubt you'd come for us," she said softly. "Not for a single moment." The simple certainty in her voice nearly broke me. She reached toward me, but I shifted slightly back, keeping my filthy hands away from her. The movement wasn't lost on her -- nothing ever was. She'd always seen me more clearly than I'd seen myself. "It's okay," she whispered, understanding in her eyes. "We're okay."

But it wasn't okay. Nothing about this was okay. My jaw clenched so hard it ached, teeth grinding together as I fought to maintain control. My family had been taken, hurt, terrified -- because of me. Because of who I was, what I did, the life I'd chosen. The blood on my hands felt suddenly symbolic, impossible to wash away.

I nodded once, sharply, the only response I could manage. My gaze never left them, cataloging every detail as if they might vanish again if I looked away -- the pallor of Yulia's skin beneath the bruising, the slight tremble in Clover's hands, the way they leaned toward each other for support. My family. Hurt but alive. Damaged but whole.

"We need to move," Hawk said from the doorway, his voice low and urgent. "Now."

I rose to my feet, body stiff from kneeling on concrete. Dr. Kestral helped Yulia stand while Cyclops supported Clover. I watched, hands hanging uselessly at my sides.

"Can you walk?" I asked them, hating how weak the question sounded. Of course they could walk. They'd survived captivity, fear and pain. They were stronger than I deserved.

"We'll manage," Yulia answered, her gaze never leaving mine. "Take us home, Salvation."

Home. The word echoed in the empty spaces inside me. I would take them home, keep them safe. And then, somehow, I would find a way to wash the blood from my hands.

* * *

The roar of motorcycles cut through the morning as we formed a protective convoy around the SUV carrying Yulia and Clover. I took point, the familiar vibration of my bike beneath me doing nothing to ease the knot in my chest. Beast and Hawk flanked the vehicle like dark sentinels, their headlights bathing the empty streets in white light. Nothing mattered except getting my family home.

Wind whipped against my face as I led the procession back to the compound. My knuckles tightened on the handlebars, the splits in my skin reopening with the pressure.

The compound appeared ahead, its outline familiar against the blue sky. Home. Safety. The massive gates stood open, waiting for us, and something tightened in my throat at the sight that greeted me. Brothers lined the entrance on both sides, standing at attention like an honor guard, solemn faces illuminated by the headlights as we passed between them. No cheers, no celebration -- just the quiet acknowledgment of what had happened, what had almost been lost.

I cut my engine outside the clubhouse, the sudden silence ringing in my ears. Around me, motorcycles went quiet one by one as my brothers parked in a protective circle around the SUV. Beast dismounted first, moving to my side with the silent communication that came from years of friendship. No words needed. He understood.

The SUV doors opened, and Dr. Kestral emerged first, circling to help Yulia and Clover. They looked even more exhausted in the harsh compound lights, their faces pale, bodies held together by sheer willpower. Yulia kept one arm around Clover's shoulders, supporting her despite her own injuries -- the fierce protectiveness that had always defined her, even when she was the one who needed protection.

"Inside," Beast ordered, his deep voice carrying across the courtyard. The single word set everything in motion -- brothers forming a corridor from the vehicle to the clubhouse, others moving to secure the perimeter, all of them focused on the same mission. Protect. Defend.

I moved toward Yulia and Clover but stopped short of touching them, painfully aware of my appearance. Blood spattered my shirt and jeans, crusted under my fingernails, mapped in the creases of my knuckles. Instead, I led the way, Beast and Hawk falling in beside me like bracketing shadows.

"Medical room's ready," Hawk said quietly. "Doc Cooper's on standby if needed. But it looks like that won't be necessary."

I nodded, the simple movement requiring more effort than it should. "Thanks."

We crossed the courtyard in silence, boots heavy

on the packed earth. Behind me, I could hear Prospero's voice, pitched low and gentle as he guided Yulia and Clover toward the clubhouse.

"Just a little farther," he was saying. "Everything's prepared. You're safe now."

The words scraped against my chest like barbed wire. Safe now. But they hadn't been safe before. I'd failed them in the most fundamental way.

The clubhouse was unusually quiet as we entered, the usual noise and chaos replaced by a watchful stillness. Brothers nodded as we passed, expressions grim, respectful.

Dr. Kestral directed us toward the infirmary -- a room we'd converted years ago for situations just like this, though never for my own family. The space was stark but well-equipped: two hospital beds with clean sheets, cabinets stocked with medical supplies, an IV stand, monitoring equipment. Too much like a hospital. Too much like defeat.

I stopped at the threshold, unable to cross into the room. My boots seemed rooted to the floor as Prospero guided Yulia to one bed, Clover to the other. Dr. Kestral moved between them with practiced efficiency, opening cabinets, preparing supplies, his movements sure and precise in a world that had suddenly lost all certainty for me.

"Get that shirt off," he instructed, snapping on latex gloves. "I need to check those ribs properly and get them wrapped."

My hand tightened on the doorframe, knuckles splitting farther as Yulia carefully removed her shirt, revealing the full extent of the bruising across her ribcage. Purple and black stained her pale skin like spilled ink, evidence of the violence she'd endured. I noticed Prospero kept his gaze locked on the opposite wall.

A presence appeared at my shoulder -- Hawk, his face lined with concern. "You should clean up," he said quietly. "Get that blood off. We've got this covered."

I shook my head, unable to look away from the scene before me. "Not yet."

"Salvation --"

"Not. Yet." Each word landed like a stone. I couldn't leave them. Couldn't take my eyes off them for even a moment. What if they disappeared again? What if this was all some cruel dream, and I'd wake to find them still missing?

Hawk retreated without another word, understanding in his silence. The respect of my brothers had never felt so heavy, so undeserved.

In the infirmary, Dr. Kestral had wrapped Yulia's ribs with practiced hands, the white bandage stark against her skin. He moved to Clover next, replacing the butterfly bandage on her cheek with a more secure dressing, his voice low and reassuring as he worked. Both of them kept glancing toward the door, toward me, their eyes seeking reassurance I couldn't give.

My shirt pulled tight across my shoulders, stiff with dried blood. My hands hung at my sides, useless, filthy things that had taken a life but failed to protect what mattered most. I wanted to go to them, to hold them, to promise that nothing like this would ever happen again. But the blood stopped me -- not just the physical stains on my skin, but the deeper stain that came with the life I'd chosen, the risks I'd brought to their door.

"Dad?" Clover's voice, small and uncertain, cut through my thoughts. "Aren't you coming in?"

I met her eyes across the room, saw the need

there, the confusion at my distance. Beside her, Yulia watched with that penetrating gaze that had always seen straight through me.

"Soon," I managed, the word scraping my throat raw. "Let the doc finish first."

It was a weak excuse. We all knew it. But I couldn't bring myself to cross that threshold, to contaminate their space with the violence that clung to me like a second skin. So I stood guard instead, a sentinel at the door, my eyes never leaving them as Dr. Kestral continued his ministrations.

Minutes stretched into an hour. My legs ached from standing, my body screaming for rest after days without sleep, but I remained motionless, watching. The doctor hooked up IVs to combat dehydration, checked vital signs, administered mild sedatives to help them rest. Through it all, Yulia's gaze kept finding mine, asking questions I had no answers for.

When he finally stepped back, pronouncing them stable but in need of rest, I felt something inside me crack. They were safe. They were home. But the distance between us -- the few steps from the doorway to their beds -- felt wider than any ocean.

My fingers twitched at my sides, wanting to reach out, to touch, to confirm they were real. Instead, I remained where I was, blood-stained and broken, watching over my family from the threshold of a room I couldn't bring myself to enter.

Chapter Nine

Salvation

The blood on my hands had dried to a flaking crust, pulling at my skin like a second hide I couldn't shed. I'd killed for them, would kill again without hesitation, but I couldn't contaminate their healing space with the evidence of that violence. So I stood guard at the door, a silent sentinel, watching over their fitful sleep until Beast had finally placed a heavy hand on my shoulder and muttered, "Go clean up, brother. They're safe now."

Hours later, the blood was gone, scrubbed away under scalding water until my skin was raw. But I still felt it there, phantom stains mapping the violence that lived in me. I'd changed into clean clothes, a simple black T-shirt and jeans, but couldn't bring myself to sleep. Every time I closed my eyes, I saw Yulia and Clover bound to those chairs, saw the knife against my daughter's cheek, saw the bruises flowering across Yulia's pale skin.

When I'd gone to check on them an hour ago, they'd been awake once more and wanting to go home. Dr. Kestral had relented and removed the IVs but made me promise to keep an eye on them and call if anything changed. I'd agreed, and now my daughter was tucked into her own bed and sleeping soundly.

I found Yulia in the living room, perched on the edge of the leather bench beneath the window. She'd changed into clean clothes… sweatpants and a soft gray T-shirt that hung loose on her frame. Her hair was still damp from a shower, pulled back from her face in a messy knot that exposed the elegant curve of her neck. She looked small, vulnerable, but her spine was straight, the core of steel that had always defined her evident even now.

She glanced up as I entered, her blue gaze tracking my movements with the watchfulness of prey that had escaped a predator but remained on high alert. The sight squeezed something in my chest -- that she should look at me that way, after eleven years under the same roof.

"Clover's still sleeping," she said, the exhaustion in her voice evident. "Dr. Kestral said she'd probably sleep at least a few more hours."

I nodded, moving to sit beside her on the bench, close but not touching. The space between us felt charged, electric with unspoken words and emotions too raw to examine.

"You should be resting too," I said, my voice rougher than intended.

"I couldn't sleep." She looked down at her hands, clasped tightly in her lap. I noticed the fresh bandages around her wrists, covering the abrasions left by the zip ties. She'd need to keep them covered so they wouldn't get infected, but since she didn't have stitches, she'd at least be able to bathe without having to keep the area dry. "Every time I closed my eyes, I was back in that room."

I understood. God, how I understood. The silence stretched between us, thick with all the things we weren't saying. How close we'd come to losing everything. How much had changed in the span of a few days. How our almost-kiss at the fair now felt like it belonged to different people in a different lifetime.

Guilt churned in my gut like acid. I should have protected them better. Should have anticipated the threat. Should have found them sooner. The thoughts circled like vultures, picking at the carcass of my failure until I shifted slightly away from her, unable to bear being so close to what I'd nearly lost through my own complacence.

Yulia's body tensed at the movement, a minute flinch that I might have missed if I hadn't been hyper-aware of her every breath. Her hands clasped tighter, knuckles going white as she tried to hide their trembling. Something in her expression shuttered, a door closing. She thought I was pulling away. And why wouldn't she? Eleven years of careful distance, of never quite crossing the line between the marriage we had on paper and the one that lived in my heart.

I noticed the way she curled in on herself as if preparing for rejection. The realization cut deeper than any knife. Even after everything, she still expected me to keep my distance.

I hesitated, the words sticking in my throat. My heart hammered against my ribs like it was trying to escape. "If you want… you can stay in my bed. Just to sleep." I kept my voice steady but inside my emotions were churning with vulnerability, need, and the fear of rejection.

Yulia's shoulders visibly relaxed, tension bleeding out of her as she processed my words. A soft smile touched her lips. Not her usual guarded smile, but something real and warm that reached her eyes.

"I'd like that," she said simply.

Three words, but they bridged the gulf between us more effectively than any grand declaration could have. I nodded, suddenly unable to speak past the tightness in my throat.

We separated without another word, Yulia heading to the bathroom while I made my way to the kitchen to get us both water. The domesticity of the task felt surreal after the recent violence, but I clung to it, a lifeline back to normalcy.

I stood in the kitchen, two glasses of water sweating on the counter beside me, thoughts circling like hungry wolves. The invitation to share my bed had slipped out, born of a desperation I hadn't fully acknowledged until the words were already hanging between us. Not sex. Just closeness. Just the certainty of knowing she was there, breathing, alive. I pressed my palms flat against the cool granite, anchoring myself to something solid while everything else felt like quicksand beneath my feet. Eleven years we'd lived as husband and wife on paper, raising Clover together, maintaining careful boundaries that suddenly seemed fragile and meaningless.

A muffled cry shattered the silence, distant but unmistakable. My body reacted before my mind processed the sound, already moving toward the hallway, heart slamming against my ribs. Clover.

Yulia emerged from the bedroom at the same moment, her hair loose and damp around her shoulders, eyes wide with the same alarm that surged through me. Our gazes locked for a fraction of a second, no words needed. Together we moved toward Clover's room, instinct propelling us forward with matching urgency.

Another cry, louder this time, the sound of my daughter trapped in terror. I hit the door first, shouldering it open without breaking stride. The bedside lamp cast a weak glow over the room, illuminating Clover's thrashing form. She'd kicked the blankets into a twisted mess, her body arching against invisible restraints, face contorted in a silent scream that occasionally broke through as desperate whimpers.

"No, please," she muttered, head tossing against the pillow. "Don't touch her. Don't --"

I reached her in three strides, lowering myself carefully onto the edge of the mattress. Her skin was clammy with cold sweat, her T-shirt clinging to her thin frame. Even in sleep, her fingers clutched at her wrists where the zip ties had left angry marks, an unconscious echo of her captivity.

"Clover." I kept my voice low, gentle, my hand hovering over her shoulder before settling with the lightest pressure. "Baby, you're safe. You're home."

She continued to struggle, caught in the grip of a nightmare more real than my presence beside her.

"Clover," I tried again, a little firmer this time. "Wake up, sweetheart. It's Dad. You're safe."

My chest ached watching her fight demons I couldn't see, couldn't protect her from. I'd always been her shield, her protector, from the moment I'd nearly lost her when she was just a little girl. Now I couldn't even guard her dreams.

I glanced back toward the doorway where Yulia hovered, uncertainty written across her features. She stood with one hand pressed against the doorframe, as if needing its support, her gaze fixed on Clover with naked concern. But she didn't approach, didn't intrude on what she perhaps saw as my territory -- comforting my daughter.

Clover's eyes flew open suddenly, wild and unfocused, pupils dilated with fear. Her breath came in rapid, shallow gasps as she struggled to orient herself.

"It's okay," I murmured, keeping my hand steady on her shoulder. "You're home. You're safe."

Recognition flickered across her face, then crumpled into relief so profound it bordered on pain. "Dad?" Her voice broke on the single syllable, splintering like glass.

"I'm here," I assured her, brushing damp hair from her forehead. "Just a nightmare. It's over now."

Clover's gaze shifted past me to where Yulia stood. "Yulia?" she called, her voice small and frightened, like the child she'd been years ago rather than the young woman she was becoming.

Yulia stepped forward hesitantly, drawn by Clover's need but still uncertain of her place in this moment.

"I'm here, *malishka*," she said softly, her accent thickening with emotion as it always did in moments of stress.

Clover reached for her with desperate fingers. "I dreamed they took us again. They hurt you and I couldn't stop them." A sob caught in her throat. "They made me watch."

Yulia moved swiftly then, crossing to the opposite side of the bed, all hesitation gone. "It was just a dream," she said, perching carefully on the edge of the mattress. "See? I am right here. The worst that happened to us was being hungry, thirsty, and some scrapes and bruises."

Clover grasped at both of us, one hand clutching my arm, the other reaching for Yulia. She looked so young, so vulnerable, with her tear-streaked face and frightened eyes. My daughter. But Yulia's too, in all the ways that mattered.

"Stay," Clover pleaded. "Both of you. Please."

I lifted the edge of the tangled blanket, a silent invitation for Yulia to join us properly on the bed. After only a moment's hesitation, she slipped beneath the covers, careful of her bruised ribs as she settled beside Clover.

I did the same on the other side, creating a

protective barrier of bodies around our daughter. The full-size bed was too small for the three of us, forcing us close together in a tangle of limbs and shared breath. Clover's smaller frame fit between us, her head tucked under my chin, her back pressed against Yulia's chest. My arm stretched across them both, hand coming to rest on Yulia's shoulder, completing the circle of protection.

"We've got you," I murmured against Clover's hair. "Nothing's going to hurt you. Not ever again."

"I was so scared," Clover whispered, her body still trembling slightly between us. "When they grabbed me at the fair, I didn't even have time to scream. And then they took Yulia too, and I thought --" She broke off, unable to voice her darkest fears.

"Shh," Yulia soothed, her hand stroking Clover's arm in slow, rhythmic motions. "We are home now. Your father found us, just as I knew he would."

"She really did know you'd come," Clover said, her fingers tightening around my arm. "She told them you would. That you'd make them sorry."

"I'll always find you," I promised, the words a vow that went beyond this moment, beyond even the kidnapping.

Gradually, Clover's breathing slowed, her body relaxing by increments as sleep reclaimed her. But this time, her dreams seemed peaceful, her face smoothing out as she nestled between us, secure in the knowledge that she was protected.

Over her head, my eyes met Yulia's in the dim light. Her hand still rested on Clover's arm, inches from where my own fingers curled around our daughter's shoulder.

My thumb moved of its own accord, tracing a small circle on Yulia's shoulder where my hand still rested. Her eyes widened slightly at the touch, but she didn't pull away. Instead, she leaned almost imperceptibly into the contact, a silent acknowledgment of something new taking shape between us.

We waited until Clover's breathing deepened into the steady rhythm of dreamless sleep before carefully extricating ourselves from the tangled sheets. I eased my arm from beneath her head while Yulia gently tucked the blanket around her shoulders. We moved like thieves in reverse, leaving something precious behind rather than taking it away. At the doorway, we both paused, looking back at the sleeping form of our daughter. She seemed younger in sleep, the stress of the past days temporarily erased from her features. I left the door cracked open just enough that we'd hear if she called out again, then followed Yulia into the dimly lit hallway.

Neither of us spoke as we made our way to my bedroom, our footsteps hushed against the worn carpet. The compound was quiet around us, the usual sounds of brotherhood -- laughter, arguing, music -- absent in deference to what we'd all been through. My door stood partially open, just as Yulia had left it when Clover's cries had pulled us away. I pushed it wider, allowing Yulia to enter first.

A single lamp burned on the nightstand, casting long shadows across the sparse furnishings. Nothing personal on the walls, no photographs, no mementos. Nothing that made it uniquely mine.

Yulia stood in the center of the room, looking smaller than usual, her arms wrapped around herself as if for protection. The lamp's glow caught the damp ends of her hair, turning the blonde strands a light copper. Even bruised and exhausted, she was the most beautiful thing I'd ever seen.

I closed the door with a soft *click*, and we stood facing each other, three feet of charged space between us. All the easy comfort we'd found in Clover's room seemed to have evaporated, replaced by an awkward tension. This was new territory. Dangerous ground.

I ran a hand through my hair, a nervous gesture I couldn't suppress. My gaze traced the visible bruises on Yulia's arms, dark smudges against her pale skin that made my stomach clench with renewed guilt. The bandages around her wrists were a stark reminder of what she'd endured.

"I should have gotten to you sooner," I said, unable to keep the words inside any longer. My voice came out rough, scraped raw by emotion. "If I'd been faster, if I'd figured it out earlier --"

Yulia stepped closer, shaking her head. "No," she said firmly. "You came. That's what matters."

The certainty in her voice staggered me. After everything -- the kidnapping, the fear, the pain -- she still had this boundless faith in me. A faith I hadn't earned, hadn't deserved.

"You don't understand," I persisted, needing her to see the weight of my failure. "They hurt you. They threatened Clover. While I was running around the city like a fucking idiot, you were --"

"Salvation." She moved closer still, close enough that I could see the flecks of darker blue in her irises, could smell the clean scent of soap on her skin. "Listen to me. I knew you would find us. I never doubted it, not for a second."

Our eyes locked in the dim light, a current passing between us that had nothing to do with the kidnapping and everything to do with eleven years of careful distance, of unspoken feelings, of a marriage that existed on paper but had somehow become real in ways neither of us had acknowledged.

"Why?" I asked, my voice barely audible. "Why did you have so much faith in me?"

Something softened in her expression, a vulnerability she rarely allowed anyone to see. "Because I know you," she said simply. "I've known you since I was sixteen years old. I've watched you raise Clover, protect the club, build this life for us. I know what kind of man you are."

The words hit me like a physical blow, breaking something loose inside my chest that had been caged for too long. Hesitantly, I raised my hand to brush a strand of hair from her face, my fingers lingering against her cheek. Her skin was warm, soft, alive beneath my touch.

Yulia leaned into my hand, her eyes fluttering closed for the briefest moment, her breath catching audibly. When she looked at me again, there was no mistaking what I saw in her gaze -- the same longing that had been building in me for years, the same need for connection that went beyond our arrangement, beyond friendship, beyond the careful boundaries we'd maintained.

Time seemed to stretch between us, seconds extending into small eternities as we stood on the precipice of something that would change everything. I traced the curve of her cheekbone with my thumb, memorizing the feel of her, anchoring myself in this moment that suddenly felt both inevitable and terrifyingly new.

"Yulia," I whispered, my voice breaking on her name.

She said nothing, but her hand came up to cover mine where it rested against her face, her fingers curling around my wrist with gentle pressure. Permission. Invitation.

I lowered my head slowly, giving her every chance to pull away, to reconsider. But she remained steady, her eyes never leaving mine until the last moment when they closed in anticipation. Our lips met in a kiss that was barely more than a whisper -- soft, tentative, questioning. A beginning rather than a culmination.

I pulled back slightly, searching her face for any sign of doubt or regret. Instead, I found only clear certainty in her eyes, a sureness that steadied my racing heart. This time when our lips met, there was nothing hesitant about it. The kiss deepened, eleven years of wanting pouring into a connection that felt like coming home after a long, lonely journey.

Her hands slid up to my shoulders, mine settling at her waist, careful of her bruised ribs. We fit together perfectly, as if our bodies had always known what our minds had been slow to accept. The kiss was both tender and urgent, gentle but with an undercurrent of need that threatened to sweep us both away.

When we finally parted, both slightly breathless, neither of us spoke. Words seemed inadequate, unnecessary in the face of what had just passed between us. Instead, Yulia's fingers found mine, intertwining with quiet certainty as we moved toward the bed. Something fundamental had shifted between us -- a truth finally acknowledged.

She winced slightly as she sat on the edge of the mattress, her hand automatically going to her bandaged ribs. I knelt before her, looking up into her face with concern.

"We don't have to --"

"I know," she interrupted. "I just want to be

close to you. To sleep knowing you're there."

I nodded, understanding completely. After the terror of separation, the fear of loss, we both needed the reassurance of proximity. Of heartbeats and breath and warmth that proved we were alive, together, safe.

The bed dipped beneath our weight as we settled side by side, not touching at first, both still navigating this new territory between us. Then Yulia turned toward me, fitting herself against my side as if she'd done it a thousand times before. My arm curved around her shoulders, drawing her closer, her head coming to rest in the hollow beneath my collarbone.

"This is real," she murmured against my chest, the words more statement than question.

I tightened my hold on her, careful of her ribs, as I pressed a kiss to the top of her head. "Yes," I promised. "This is real."

In the dim light of the single lamp, with Yulia's warmth seeping into my bones and her heartbeat steady against me, I finally felt the knot of tension in my chest begin to unravel. We still had healing to do, all of us. There were conversations to be had, fears to be faced, a future to be rebuilt. But for now, for this moment, it was enough to hold her close and know that tomorrow, for the first time in eleven years, we would wake as true husband and wife.

Chapter Ten

Salvation

I couldn't sleep, even with Yulia's warmth pressed against me. Eleven years of wanting, of holding back, of telling myself this was enough -- and now she was here, in my bed, her breath steady against my chest. But nothing had been said, not really. "This is real" wasn't enough after everything we'd been through. She deserved more than that. She deserved the whole truth, even if speaking it aloud terrified me more than facing down armed men ever had.

I shifted carefully, not wanting to disturb her, but she wasn't asleep either. Her eyes opened, finding mine in the dim light, questioning.

"I'm going to get some water," I murmured, needing a moment to collect my thoughts. "Do you want anything?"

She shook her head, her dark blonde hair spilling across my pillow as I eased away from her. The floor was cold against my bare feet as I moved to the bathroom, splashing water on my face and staring at my reflection in the mirror. The man who looked back at me seemed older, harder than the one who'd first brought a sixteen-year-old Yulia to live under his protection all those years ago.

When I returned, she'd sat up against the headboard, the sheet pulled up to cover herself. Something in her posture -- a new wariness, a subtle withdrawal -- told me she'd misinterpreted my leaving. Which meant I needed to forget my trek to the kitchen and stay here. There was too much left unsaid between us, and I knew waiting any longer would be a mistake.

I sat on the edge of the bed, my back to her at first, hands clasped between my knees to hide their trembling. The silence stretched between us, heavy with unspoken words.

"Salvation?" Her voice was soft, uncertain. "What is it?"

"I don't know how to say this." My voice sounded rougher than I intended, edged with emotions too long contained.

"Say what?" A hint of fear colored her question, and I realized she might be thinking the worst -- that I regretted our kiss, that I was about to pull away again.

I forced myself to turn, to look at her directly. My throat tightened.

"I want this to be real," I finally managed. "Not just because of what happened."

Her eyes widened slightly, her lips parting in surprise.

"I want a real marriage," I continued, the words coming easier now that I'd started. "I have for years. I just… I didn't know how to tell you. Didn't know if that was what you wanted. Or if I would end up scaring you and making you want to run from me."

My hands were definitely shaking now, so I clenched them tighter. What kind of bad-ass biker got all emotional like this? If my brothers could see me now… I took a breath to steady myself.

"When they took you -- when I thought I might never see you again -- I realized what a fucking coward I've been. Eleven years, Yulia. Eleven years of living with you, raising Clover with you, wanting you, and never having the guts to just say it. Well, not those first few years. I'm not a sick bastard who thought of a broken teenager that way. It wasn't until later, when you were about twenty, that I started seeing you differently."

She hadn't moved, hadn't spoken, her face frozen in an expression I couldn't quite read. Had I misunderstood the meaning of our kiss? Had I completely misjudged what was happening between us?

"If you don't feel the same," I said quickly, "nothing has to change. We can go back to how things were. I just needed you to know --"

"Salvation. Kye." My name on her lips stopped me cold. Her voice trembled, thick with emotion. "I have wanted that for so long I can't remember when it started."

For a moment, I couldn't breathe, couldn't think. "What?"

She shifted forward, wincing slightly as the movement pulled at her bruised ribs, but determined nonetheless. "I have been in love with you for years," she said, her accent more pronounced with emotion. "I just never thought… I was afraid…"

Her hand reached for mine, fingers sliding between my own, the simple contact sending electricity up my arm. "I thought you saw me as an obligation. A responsibility. The damaged girl you had to protect."

"No." I squeezed her fingers, anchoring myself to her touch. "Never that. Not for a long time.

"One day I looked at you, really looked at you, and realized you weren't that scared girl anymore. You were a woman. Strong. Beautiful." I swallowed hard. "And I realized I didn't just want to protect you. I wanted you. All of you."

Her free hand came up to touch my face, fingertips tracing the line of my jaw with wonder. "I was so afraid to tell you," she admitted. "I thought you might ask me to leave. That it would make things awkward between us, or worse, that you would feel obligated because of our arrangement."

"I was afraid too," I confessed, leaning into her touch. "That I'd scare you. That after everything you'd been through, the last thing you'd want was for things to change between us. That I'd be taking advantage."

A small, incredulous laugh escaped her. "We've been such fools."

"Complete idiots," I agreed, a smile tugging at my lips despite the intensity of the moment.

I raised our joined hands, pressing my lips to her knuckles. "I'm sorry it took nearly losing you to make me brave enough to say it."

"Don't be sorry," she whispered. "Just don't stop saying it."

Something broke loose in my chest then, a dam bursting after years of careful containment. I leaned forward, my free hand coming up to cradle her face, and kissed her properly -- years of wanting poured into a single connection.

She responded immediately, her fingers tightening around mine, her other hand sliding to the back of my neck to pull me closer. The kiss deepened, her lips parting beneath mine, a small sound escaping her throat that nearly undid me completely.

When we finally broke apart, both breathing harder, I rested my forehead against hers. Relief washed over me in waves so powerful I felt almost dizzy with it. Her eyes were bright with unshed tears, but her smile -- God, her smile -- was like nothing I'd ever seen before. Open. Unguarded. Real.

"I love you," I said, testing the words that had lived in my heart for so long. "I love you, Yulia."

Her smile widened, tears spilling over now to

track down her cheeks. "I love you too," she whispered against my lips. "I have for so long."

I brushed away her tears with my thumb, marveling at the softness of her skin, at the fact I could touch her like this now. No more holding back. No more pretending. Just us, finally honest with each other after all these years.

"So what happens now?" she asked, her gaze never leaving mine.

I smiled, feeling lighter than I had in years, maybe ever. "Now we start over. A real marriage. No more separate rooms. No more careful distance."

"I'd like that," she said, her fingers tracing patterns on the back of my hand. "Very much."

I kissed her again, softly this time, a promise rather than a passion. "We have time," I murmured against her lips. "All the time in the world."

But even as I said it, I knew time wasn't what I wanted right now. We'd already wasted so much of it. The air between us changed, charged with years of restraint finally breaking. I kissed Yulia again, but this time there was nothing tentative about it. My hands moved to cup her face, thumbs brushing along her cheekbones with a reverence that belied the hunger building inside me. Her response was immediate, her fingers digging into my shoulders, pulling me closer until our bodies pressed together through the thin fabric of our clothes.

"I want you," I murmured against her lips, the words both a confession and a question.

"Yes," she breathed. "I've wanted this for so long."

That simple admission nearly undid me. I deepened the kiss, one hand sliding into her hair while the other traced down her neck, her shoulder, coming to rest at her waist. Her skin was warm beneath my palm where her shirt had ridden up, but I hesitated, suddenly aware of her injuries.

"Your ribs," I reminded her, pulling back slightly to study her face. "I don't want to hurt you."

A small, determined smile curved her lips. "Then be gentle," she said. "But don't stop."

She reached for the hem of her T-shirt, wincing slightly as she began to lift it. I caught her hands, stopping her.

"Let me," I said softly.

With careful movements, I eased the shirt up and over her head, my breath catching at the sight of her. White bandages wrapped around her ribs, stark against her pale skin. Bruises bloomed across her collarbone and her upper arms, ones I hadn't noticed when we'd rescued her. Which meant they'd likely shown up after we'd gotten home. The evidence of what she'd endured made my throat tighten with a complex mixture of rage and tenderness.

I traced my fingertips lightly over a bruise on her shoulder, barely making contact. "Does it hurt?"

"Not anymore," she answered, her blue eyes never leaving mine. "Not when you touch me."

My own shirt followed hers, dropped carelessly to the floor. Yulia's hands explored newly exposed skin with a hesitant wonder that made my heart race. Her fingers traced the lines of my tattoos, the scars earned over years with the club, mapping me like territory she'd longed to claim.

When her hands reached for the waistband of my jeans, I caught them gently, bringing them to my lips.

"Are you sure?" I asked, needing her absolute certainty. "We can wait. Until you're healed. Until --"

"I don't want to wait anymore," she interrupted,

a fierceness in her voice I rarely heard.

To emphasize her point, she guided one of my hands to her breast, her eyes closing briefly at the contact. The trust in that gesture -- after everything she'd been through, both recently and years ago -- humbled me.

"Tell me if anything hurts," I insisted, carefully lowering her back onto the pillows. "Promise me."

"I promise," she whispered, reaching up to pull me down for another kiss.

I took my time, learning her body with a reverence that bordered on worship. Every touch, every kiss was measured, deliberate -- mindful of her injuries but determined to show her exactly how much I wanted her. Her bandaged wrists, her bruised ribs, the bruises along her skin -- I kissed each one with a tenderness I hadn't known I possessed, as if I could erase the pain with nothing but my lips.

Yulia's breathing quickened as my hands and mouth explored her body, small sounds escaping her that drove me to the edge of my control. When my fingers found the waistband of her sweatpants, her hips lifted in silent invitation.

"You're beautiful," I told her as I eased the fabric down her legs. "So fucking beautiful."

A flush spread across her cheeks at my words, but she didn't look away. Instead, her hands reached for me, tugging at my remaining clothes with growing urgency. "I need to feel you," she said, her voice low and insistent. "All of you."

We shed the last barriers between us, and I paused for a moment, taking in the sight of her beneath me -- my wife, finally, in every sense of the word. Her hair spilled across my pillow, her blue eyes dark with desire, her body marked by violence but still perfect to me. Mine to protect. Mine to cherish.

I reached between us, sliding my fingers along the lips of her pussy, feeling how wet she already was. Parting the lips, I teased her clit, using small, light strokes. She gasped and her eyes half-closed as she bit her lip. Watching the pleasure etched on her features made me harder than before. I eased a finger inside her, testing how tight she was. Yulia whimpered and reached for me, her nails biting into my arms, as if begging me not to stop.

I used my thumb to rub her clit as I thrust my finger, slowly, wanting to draw out her pleasure for as long as possible. I felt her get hotter. Wetter. And I knew it wouldn't be long before she was coming. My heart thundered in my chest as I watched her, and when she came apart, crying out softly, my cock twitched and I knew I needed to be inside her. I kicked out of my jeans.

I was as gentle as I could be as I settled between her splayed thighs and pressed my cock against her pussy, slowly sinking into her. We both gasped at the sensation. Her fingers dug into my shoulders, her body arching toward mine despite her injuries. I moved slowly at first, watching her face for any sign of pain.

"Okay?" I managed to ask, fighting for control.

"More than okay," she assured me, her legs wrapping around my hips to pull me deeper. "I've never felt anything so incredible in my life."

We found our rhythm together, the rustle of sheets and our mingled breaths the only sounds in the room. My forehead pressed against hers, our gazes locked, nothing hidden between us anymore. Her hands traced paths of fire across my back, my shoulders, urging me on while I fought to maintain control, to keep my movements gentle despite the growing urgency I felt.

"You won't break me," she whispered against my ear, understanding my struggle. "I'm stronger than I look."

Something snapped inside me at her words -- not my control, but the last of my hesitation. I kissed her deeply, my movements becoming more insistent, more demanding, though still mindful of her injuries. Her response was immediate, her body rising to meet mine, her soft cries of pleasure the most beautiful sound I'd ever heard.

I watched her come apart in my arms, her eyes widening with surprise and pleasure, my name on her lips like a prayer. The sight of her -- uninhibited, trusting, mine -- pushed me over the edge moments later, my release hitting me with an intensity that left me shaking.

Afterward, we lay tangled together, her head on my chest, my fingers tracing lazy patterns on her shoulder. Her breath came in soft puffs against my skin, her body relaxed and warm against mine. Neither of us spoke immediately, content to exist in the afterglow of something that had been building for years.

"Are you okay?" I finally asked, pressing a kiss to the top of her head. "Your ribs?"

She smiled against my chest. "I'm perfect. Better than I've ever been."

I tightened my arms around her, careful of her bruises but needing to hold her close. The simple pleasure of having her naked in my bed, of being able to touch her freely, to kiss her whenever I wanted -- it felt like a gift I'd never expected to receive.

"I can't believe we waited so long," I said, the regret evident in my voice despite the contentment flowing through me.

Yulia raised her head to look at me, her expression serious. "Perhaps we needed that time. For me to heal. For us to build trust. For Clover to grow up with stability. And for you to get over the loss of Clover's mother." She traced my jawline with one finger. I hadn't shaved in a few days and her finger scraped over my whiskers. "Maybe we found each other exactly when we were meant to."

I caught her hand, pressing a kiss to her palm. "When did you get so wise?"

"I've had a good teacher," she said with a small smile. "A man who taught me patience, strength, loyalty. A man who showed me what love looks like, even when he couldn't say the words."

Something warm expanded in my chest, pushing against my ribs as if my heart had grown too large to contain. "I love you," I said, the words coming easier now. "I'll spend the rest of my life making up for all the times I should have said it but didn't."

"We have time," she reminded me, settling back against my chest. "All the time in the world."

I held her close as her breathing deepened toward sleep, marveling at how completely everything had changed. The woman in my arms was no longer just my wife on paper, no longer just Clover's mother-figure, no longer just my roommate and friend. She was my partner in every sense -- the other half of something I hadn't even realized was incomplete until now. Whatever came next -- the continued healing from their ordeal, telling Clover about the change in our relationship, facing the world as a true couple -- we would handle it together. No more holding back. No more pretending. Just us, finally whole after years of waiting.

Chapter Eleven

Salvation

I woke to an empty bed, my hand instinctively reaching for Yulia before my eyes even opened. The sheets beside me were still warm, her scent lingering on the pillow. For one disorienting moment, panic flared in my chest -- the same blind terror I'd felt when she and Clover had disappeared from the fairgrounds. Then reality settled back in. We were home. They were safe. And after eleven years of marriage on paper, Yulia and I had finally crossed the line we'd danced around for so long.

I sat up, running a hand through my hair as I listened for sounds in the house. The shower wasn't running. No clatter of dishes from the kitchen. Just the familiar ambient noise of the compound filtering through the windows -- distant voices, motorcycles rumbling to life, the rhythmic clang of weights from the club gym.

A folded piece of paper on Yulia's pillow caught my eye. I reached for it, recognizing Hawk's messy scrawl immediately.

Salvation -- Hayley's got Clover for the day. Teaching her to bake or some shit. Take your woman somewhere nice. Bikes are gassed up. Don't fuck this up. -- H

A postscript in different handwriting -- Hayley's, I assumed -- added: *The blue helmet in the garage is Yulia's size. You're welcome.*

Then one more, this one from my daughter: *Take her somewhere nice and don't worry about me. She's having breakfast with Ranger and Danica.*

I stared at the note, a slow smile spreading across

my face. Hawk and Hayley, playing matchmaker. As if Yulia and I needed the push after last night. Still, the thought of a day with just the two of us, away from the compound, away from reminders of what we'd just been through… my chest tightened with something that felt like anticipation mixed with anxiety.

Our first real date. Eleven years into our marriage.

I showered quickly and dressed in my usual jeans and black T-shirt, before shrugging into my cut. The compound was alive with morning activity as I made my way to the garage. The smell of coffee drifted from the kitchen and I paused to pour a cup, taking a sip as I stared out the small window over the sink. Everything normal. Everything as it should be.

Except nothing was normal anymore. Not since I'd finally told Yulia the truth. Not since she'd said she loved me too.

The thought sent a jolt through me that was equal parts terror and exhilaration. I'd faced down rival clubs without flinching, had killed men who threatened what was mine, but this -- this fragile, newborn thing between Yulia and me -- terrified me in ways I couldn't articulate. I drained the cup and placed it in the sink.

The garage was cool and dim compared to the brightness outside. My bike waited in its usual spot, the sleek black Harley a familiar comfort. Beside it stood Yulia's bike -- an older model I'd taught her to ride years ago, but that she rarely used. I ran my hands over both machines, checking them with the methodical precision that came from years of riding.

Oil levels. Tire pressure. Brakes. Chain tension. I lost myself in the familiar routine, the smell of grease and metal grounding me in the present moment.

"Good morning."

Her voice from the doorway of the open garage sent a ripple down my spine. I straightened, wiping my hands on a shop rag as I turned to face her.

Yulia stood framed in the entrance, backlit by morning sun. She wore black riding jeans that hugged her curves and a leather jacket I'd never seen before -- fitted, feminine, but unmistakably protective. I noticed something else about it… the Reckless Kings colors on the front in a small patch. It made me wonder where she'd gotten it, since I hadn't seen one like it before.

"Morning," I managed, suddenly unsure what to do with my hands. Before last night, I would have nodded, kept my distance. Now? Everything was different, the rules rewritten.

She solved the problem by crossing to me, rising on tiptoes to press a kiss to my jaw. "Hawk and Hayley sent me to Ranger's house for breakfast, so I figured they had something planned. Danica gave this jacket to me, as a gift from the club."

"They're not exactly subtle, but I can't say I dislike their plan of setting us up on a date," I said, allowing my hand to settle at her waist, still marveling that I could touch her like this now. "How are your ribs?"

"Better. Still sore, but the wrapping helps." She glanced at the bikes. "Are we going somewhere?"

I nodded, my thumb tracing small circles against her leather-clad hip. "I thought we could. If you're up for it." I hesitated, suddenly feeling like a teenager with his first crush instead of a grown man with his wife. "I thought we could ride through the hills, maybe stop somewhere special."

Her smile widened, the slight reserve in her expression melting away. "I'd like that."

I reached past her for the blue helmet hanging on the wall -- the one Hayley had somehow procured in Yulia's size. The one I'd bought for her previously had vanished at some point. "Try this on."

She took it, turning it in her hands before slipping it over her head. It fit perfectly, framing her face in a way that emphasized her high cheekbones and blue eyes. Even with most of her features hidden, she was the most beautiful thing I'd ever seen.

"How do I look?" she asked, her voice muffled slightly by the helmet.

"Perfect," I said simply.

A faint blush colored her cheeks as she removed the helmet. "It's been a while since I've ridden. You might need to go slow."

"We've got all day," I assured her, resisting the urge to pull her against me again. If I started kissing her now, we might never make it out of the garage.

Instead, I focused on final preparations, and explaining the route I had in mind. Yulia listened attentively, asking questions about road conditions and how long we'd be gone. The conversation was ordinary, practical -- the kind we might have had before. But the undercurrent had changed, electricity running beneath every exchanged glance, every casual touch.

"Ready?" I asked finally, swinging my leg over my bike.

Yulia nodded, settling onto her own machine with a grace that belied her claimed rustiness. She'd always been a natural on a bike, though she rarely indulged. Something about the way she straddled the seat, her back straight and hands confident on the grips, sent heat spreading through my chest. That's when I noticed the back of her jacket. It was the same as her property cut and said *Property of Salvation*.

I started my engine, the familiar rumble vibrating up through my bones. Yulia followed suit, her smaller bike purring to life beneath her. She flashed me a smile that was equal parts excitement and nervousness, then lowered her visor.

I led the way out of the garage, across the compound toward the main gates. In my mirrors, I could see Yulia following, her form compact and perfect on the bike. Pride swelled in my chest at the sight -- my wife, my woman, riding with me. No longer just a name on paper or a responsibility to protect, but a partner. My partner.

The gates swung open as we approached, the brothers on security detail nodding as we passed. I throttled up as we hit the open road, but kept my speed moderate, constantly checking my mirrors to ensure Yulia was comfortable with the pace. Her riding was smooth, confident, and I felt myself relaxing incrementally as we put distance between ourselves and the compound.

For the first time in days -- maybe years -- I felt something like freedom unfurling in my chest. The road stretched before us, Yulia rode safely behind me, and we had a whole day just to be together. To figure out what this new reality meant for both of us.

I gunned the engine, feeling Yulia do the same behind me as we roared toward the distant hills, leaving the shadows of the past week behind us -- at least for today.

The road climbed steadily through pine forests, unspooling before us like a ribbon of black silk against the green. Yulia had pulled up beside me, and I kept an eye on her as she leaned into each curve with growing confidence. The farther we got from the compound, the more her body language changed -- shoulders relaxing, head tilting up to take in the scenery flashing past. Freedom looked good on her. It always had, from the first tentative steps she'd taken away from her trauma all those years ago to now, following me up mountain roads with the kind of grace that couldn't be taught.

Wind buffeted my body as we accelerated around a sweeping bend, the valley opening up on our right side. Sunlight dappled the asphalt through breaks in the tree canopy, creating patterns of light and shadow that blurred beneath our wheels. The familiar vibration of the engine between my legs, the smell of pine and wildflowers, the occasional flash of wildlife darting into the underbrush -- everything felt heightened, more vivid than usual.

Or maybe it was just that Yulia was with me, really with me, for the first time.

I watched her take a curve perfectly, her body shifting with the bike as if they were a single entity. Her earlier claim about being rusty was clearly false modesty. She rode like she'd been born to it, like the machine was an extension of herself. My chest tightened at the sight, pride and something fiercer, more possessive, surging through me. Most of our old ladies didn't ride, but Brick had suggested it might be a good way for her to heal, and she'd taken to it well.

We'd ridden together before, of course. Brief trips to town, or a quick jaunt down the highway. But never like this -- never as a couple, never with the knowledge of how her skin felt against mine, how her lips tasted, how she whispered my name in the darkness. The memories from last night sent heat spreading through me that had nothing to do with the sun beating down on my leather cut.

The road twisted higher. Eventually, I spotted

what I'd been looking for -- a small turnout perched on the mountainside, offering an unobstructed view of the landscape below. I signaled to Yulia and began to slow, guiding my bike off the main road and onto the gravel turnout.

We parked side by side at the edge of the clearing, kickstands down, engines cooling with metallic ticks in the mountain silence. Below us stretched the valley in panorama -- a town nestled against the river, distant farms creating patchwork patterns of green and gold, and beyond it all, the compound, just visible as a cluster of buildings.

Yulia removed her helmet, shaking out her hair with a small, breathless laugh. Her cheeks were flushed from the ride, her eyes bright with exhilaration. She'd never looked more beautiful.

"That was amazing," she said, setting her helmet on the seat. "I'd forgotten how good it feels."

I pulled off my own helmet, running a hand through my flattened hair. "You ride like you never stopped."

She ducked her head slightly at the compliment, but I caught her smile. "It comes back to you. Like muscle memory."

We moved to the low stone wall that bordered the turnout, standing side by side as we looked out over the valley. The morning sun warmed the left sides of our faces, while a cool mountain breeze kept the heat manageable. Birds called to each other from the trees behind us. For a long moment, we just stood there, shoulders almost touching, absorbing the peace of the moment.

"Thank you for bringing me here," Yulia said finally, her voice soft.

I glanced at her, taking in her profile against the

backdrop of sky and distant mountains. "I used to come here to think. When things got complicated with the club, or when…" I hesitated, then decided on honesty. "When I needed to get away from how I felt about you."

She turned to me then, surprise and something deeper in her eyes. "You came here because of me?"

"More times than I can count." I shrugged, a gesture that felt inadequate for the weight of the admission. "Especially in the last few years. When pretending was getting too hard."

Yulia's hand found mine, her fingers sliding between my own with a confidence that was still new, still thrilling. "We wasted so much time," she murmured.

"No." I squeezed her hand gently. "We weren't ready before. You needed to heal. I needed to learn patience." I paused, then added, "Clover needed stability."

Her lips curved into a small smile. "And now?"

"Now we're here." I brought our joined hands to my lips, pressing a kiss to her knuckles. "Together. Finally."

Her eyes softened at the gesture, the reserve that had been part of her for so long melting away by degrees. She leaned against me slightly, and I released her hand to wrap my arm around her shoulders instead, drawing her closer to my side.

We stood like that for several minutes, watching a hawk circle lazily above the valley floor. The silence between us was comfortable, charged with potential rather than awkwardness. I found myself thinking about all the moments like this we could have in the future -- all the ordinary minutes made extraordinary simply because we were sharing them.

My gaze drifted to the town below, following the main street until I could just make out a particular storefront. A plan that had been forming in my mind since dawn crystallized into certainty.

"See that building there?" I pointed toward the town. "The one with the blue awning?"

Yulia squinted, following my gesture. "I think so."

"It's a jewelry store." I turned to face her, suddenly nervous but determined. "I want to get you a proper ring."

She blinked, her hand automatically moving to the plain gold band she'd worn for eleven years -- the one I'd slipped onto her finger during our courthouse ceremony when she was barely more than a girl. Her expression clouded slightly as she touched it.

"What's wrong with this one?" she asked, a hint of uncertainty in her voice.

I caught her hand, running my thumb over the simple band. "Nothing. But it was part of our arrangement. Our protection plan." I met her eyes steadily. "You deserve better than what I gave you back then. This is real now."

Something flickered across her face -- surprise, followed by a softening around her eyes that made my heart stutter in my chest.

"You don't have to," she said, but I could tell the idea pleased her.

"I want to." I pressed another kiss to her knuckles. "I want everyone to look at your hand and know you're not just protected. You're loved."

The word still felt new on my tongue, but it came easier each time. Yulia's eyes brightened with unshed tears, but her smile was radiant.

"Then yes," she said simply. "I'd like that."

I pulled her closer, kissing her properly this time -- a slow, deep kiss that held promise and certainty and the future all at once. When we broke apart, her cheeks were flushed again, but not from the ride.

"Ready?" I asked, nodding toward our bikes.

She nodded, squeezing my hand once more before releasing it. We walked back to the motorcycles, and I couldn't help but notice the spring in her step, the new lightness in her movements. As we donned our helmets and fired up the engines, I caught her eye through her open visor and saw the same anticipation reflected there that I felt coursing through my own veins.

We pulled back onto the mountain road, angling downward now toward the town and what waited for us there. Not just a ring, but a first step into the life we should have been living all along.

* * *

The jewelry store looked smaller from the outside than I remembered, tucked between a bakery and a bookshop on the town's main street. Its blue awning fluttered slightly in the breeze, gold lettering spelling out *Hartman's Fine Jewelry* in an elegant script that had faded with time. We parked our bikes at the curb, and I kicked down the stand on mine before moving to help Yulia with hers. She removed her helmet, hair tumbling free around her shoulders, and I caught the momentary flash of uncertainty in her eyes as she looked up at the storefront.

"You've been here before?" she asked, smoothing her wind-tangled hair with one hand.

I nodded, taking her helmet and securing it to her bike. "A few times. For club business." I didn't elaborate that those visits had involved pawning items we'd acquired through less-than-legal means. Some parts of club life were better left unshared, even with her.

Yulia's fingers fidgeted with the plain gold band on her left hand, twisting it nervously. I covered her hand with mine, stilling the movement.

"We don't have to do this today," I said quietly. "If you're not ready."

She shook her head, a determined set to her jaw that I recognized. "No, I want to. It's just..." She glanced down at her riding gear, then back at the store with its polished windows and tasteful displays. "I'm not dressed for this."

I laughed softly, gesturing to my own leather cut with its patches. "Neither am I. But our money spends the same as anyone else's."

That earned me a small smile, though the tension didn't completely leave her shoulders. I took her hand, threading our fingers together in a way that still felt new and thrilling, and led her to the door. The small brass bell above it chimed as we entered, announcing our presence to the empty shop.

Inside, the store was cool and quiet, the air scented faintly with polish and leather. Glass cases lined three walls, their contents glittering under recessed lighting. The floor was dark hardwood, worn smooth by decades of customers, and soft classical music played from hidden speakers. It felt like stepping into another world -- one far removed from the compound, from motorcycles and club business, from the violence that had touched our lives just days ago.

A door behind the counter opened, and an elderly man with wire-rimmed glasses and neatly combed silver hair emerged. He paused momentarily at the sight of us -- taking in my cut, the tattoos visible on my forearms -- but recovered quickly, professional smile firmly in place. He wasn't the man I usually dealt with, but I could tell he was in charge.

"Good morning," he greeted us, his voice cultured but not unfriendly. "Welcome to Hartman's. I'm Arthur Hartman. How may I assist you today?"

I felt Yulia's hand tighten slightly in mine, her discomfort palpable. Before I could speak, she surprised me by stepping forward.

"We're looking for a ring," she said, her accent more pronounced than usual, as it often was when she was nervous. "A wedding ring."

Arthur's eyes flicked to the plain band on her finger, then to our joined hands, understanding dawning in his gaze. "Of course. Something to replace the current one, perhaps?"

I nodded. "Something special."

He gestured toward a case on the right side of the store. "Why don't we start over here? I have several lovely options that might interest you."

We followed him to the case, where dozens of rings glittered against black velvet -- some simple bands, others elaborate confections of precious metals and gemstones. Yulia's eyes widened slightly at the display.

"See anything you like?" I asked, watching her reaction carefully.

She bit her lower lip, gaze moving uncertainly over the options. "Maybe something simple?" Her finger pointed to a plain platinum band, only marginally more elaborate than what she already wore. "This one is fine."

Arthur removed the ring she'd indicated, placing it on a small velvet pad for her to examine. But I shook my head slightly.

"Let's look at some others first," I suggested. "Something with a stone, maybe."

Yulia's eyes met mine, a hint of panic in them. "Salvation, really, I don't need anything fancy. This is more than enough."

I understood her reluctance. For a girl who'd grown up in the cold opulence of her father's Bratva connections, who'd been taught that beauty was just another form of currency, accepting something purely decorative, purely for pleasure, wouldn't come easily. She'd spent so long focusing on survival, on practicality, that asking for something simply because it was beautiful felt foreign to her. To most, she would have appeared to be a spoiled princess, but I had a feeling there was quite a bit we didn't know about her time with her family. Even though Grimm's wife was her sister, I wasn't convinced she'd told him absolutely everything either. Our women seemed to pick up pretty quick that we were on overprotective lot.

"This isn't about what you need," I said quietly, tucking a strand of hair behind her ear. "It's about what you deserve."

Her eyes softened at my words, though uncertainty still lingered in their blue depths. Arthur, sensing the delicacy of the moment, tactfully moved a few steps away, pretending to adjust another display.

"Let me do this for you," I continued, keeping my voice low, just for her. "Let me give you something that shows the world what you mean to me."

After a long moment, she nodded, a small but significant surrender. "Okay."

Arthur returned at my gesture, and I explained what we were looking for -- something unique, elegant but not ostentatious, with character.

"I think I might have just the thing," he said,

retreating to a cabinet behind the counter. He returned with a black velvet tray bearing rings that hadn't been in the display cases -- special pieces, I guessed, or custom work.

"These are some of my personal designs," he explained, setting the tray on the counter before us. "One-of-a-kind pieces."

The rings were indeed distinctive -- each clearly crafted with artistic vision rather than mass production in mind. Some were bold designs in mixed metals. Others featured unusual stone settings or intricate metalwork. But my attention was immediately drawn to one in the corner of the tray.

It was a band of rose gold, delicate but substantial, with tiny roses engraved around its circumference, so detailed I could make out individual petals and leaves. Set within the center of one rose was a small pink diamond that caught the light with unexpected fire.

I picked it up without hesitation, something in my chest tightening as I examined it. "This one."

Yulia leaned closer, her breath catching audibly as she saw the ring in my palm. Her finger reached out to trace one of the tiny roses, the gesture almost reverent.

"It's beautiful," she whispered.

"It reminds me of you," I said, the words simple but loaded with meaning. "Beautiful. Strong. With hidden depths."

Her eyes lifted to mine, wide and suddenly bright with unshed tears. Arthur discreetly turned away again, giving us privacy in the moment.

"May I?" I asked, nodding toward her left hand with its simple band.

Yulia nodded, extending her hand toward me.

With careful fingers, I slid the plain gold band from her finger. I pocketed it, knowing we'd keep it as a reminder of where we'd started, then took the rose-engraved ring and held it poised at the tip of her finger.

"Yulia Romanov," I said softly, using her maiden name deliberately, "will you be my wife? For real this time?"

A single tear escaped, tracking down her cheek as she nodded. "Yes," she whispered. "Yes."

I slid the ring onto her finger, where it settled as if it had been made for her. The pink diamond caught the light, sending tiny reflections dancing across her skin. Yulia stared at it, wonder in her expression that made my heart clench painfully in my chest.

"It's perfect," she said, her voice barely audible.

I lifted her hand to my lips, pressing a kiss just above where the ring now sat. "Yes," I agreed. "It is."

Arthur returned with impeccable timing, smiling at Yulia's obvious pleasure. "It suits you beautifully," he said. "As if it were made for your hand."

We completed the purchase with minimal fuss -- the price was steep but not unexpected, and I handed over my credit card without hesitation. The club paid its members well, and I'd never been one for extravagant spending. Until now. Until her.

As we stepped back out into the sunshine, Yulia kept looking at her hand, turning it this way and that to watch how the light played across the pink diamond and the detailed engravings. Her expression was one of disbelief mixed with joy, as if she couldn't quite process that the beautiful object now belonged to her.

"Thank you," she said as we reached our bikes, her eyes meeting mine with an openness I'd rarely seen before. "Not just for the ring. For…" She struggled to find the words.

"I know," I said, pulling her close for a moment. "Me too."

And I did know. This wasn't about the ring itself. It was about worth. About belonging. About turning a paper arrangement into something real and solid and permanent.

As we mounted our bikes to head back to the compound, I caught her stealing one more glance at her hand, a smile playing at the corners of her mouth that was worth more than all the diamonds in that store.

Chapter Twelve

Salvation
Two Weeks Later

I stood in the kitchen doorway, watching Yulia fold Clover's clothes into an overnight bag, her movements precise despite the slight tremor in her hands. Our daughter had been bouncing off the walls with excitement when Cyclops offered to have her stay at his place for the weekend -- something about teaching her to work on engines and letting her hang out with his kids. Her excitement had made it difficult for her to focus on a task for more than a minute. The timing of Cyclops' offer felt deliberate, but I wasn't complaining.

"She has everything she needs?" I asked, moving closer to where Yulia worked at the kitchen table.

"Toothbrush, clean clothes, her phone charger." Yulia's accent was softer than usual, the way it got when she was nervous or thinking too hard about something. "Cyclops said they might go to the movies tonight."

I nodded, but my attention wasn't really on Clover's weekend plans. It was on the way Yulia's hair caught the afternoon light streaming through our windows, on the curve of her neck as she bent over the bag, on the new ease between us since we'd finally stopped pretending our marriage was just paperwork.

Two weeks. Two weeks since I'd slipped that rose-gold ring onto her finger and we'd admitted what had been building between us for years. Two weeks of falling asleep with her in my arms, of waking up to her smile, of small touches and stolen kisses that still felt like miracles.

"There." She zipped the bag closed. "All set."

The sound of a motorcycle in the driveway announced Cyclops's arrival. Through the window, I watched him park his bike and remove his helmet, his movements unhurried. He caught sight of me through the glass and raised a hand in greeting, that knowing smirk on his face that told me everyone in the club was perfectly aware of what they were doing by giving us this time alone.

Clover burst through the door moments later, practically vibrating with energy. "Is he here? Are we leaving now? Did you pack my --"

"Everything's ready," Yulia interrupted gently, handing over the overnight bag. "Be good for Cyclops. Listen to what he tells you."

Clover rolled her eyes but her grin was infectious. "I'm sixteen, not seven." She hugged Yulia quickly, then moved to me. "Don't do anything I wouldn't do while I'm gone," she said with a wicked gleam in her eyes that reminded me exactly how much she'd grown up.

"Get out of here, kid," I said, ruffling her dark hair. But I was smiling as I said it.

She grabbed her bag and bounded toward the door, then paused on the threshold. "You two should, you know, relax. Maybe stay in bed all day or something." The innocent tone didn't fool anyone.

Heat flushed through me at Clover's words, but before I could respond, she was gone, the door slamming behind her with typical teenage exuberance. Through the window, I watched her practically skip to Cyclops's bike, chattering animatedly as he helped her secure her bag.

"She's not subtle," Yulia said softly behind me,

but when I turned, her cheeks were pink.

"None of them are." I moved closer, drawn by the flush in her skin, by the way she was worrying her lower lip between her teeth. "Does that bother you?"

She shook her head, but didn't quite meet my eyes. "It's just... we have the whole weekend. Just us."

The weight of that settled between us. Forty-eight hours with no interruptions, no club business, no teenager bursting through the door at unexpected moments. Just Yulia and me, finally free to explore this new reality without holding back.

I reached for her, my hands settling at her waist, thumbs tracing small circles through the fabric of her shirt. "What do you want to do?"

Her blue eyes lifted to mine, and the heat I saw there made my breath catch. "I want you to take me to bed," she said, her voice barely above a whisper. "And I want you to keep me there."

The honesty in her words, the direct way she looked at me as she said them, sent electricity shooting down my spine. This was still new territory for us -- being able to want each other openly, without hesitation.

"You sure?" I asked, needing to hear it again.

Instead of answering with words, she rose on her toes and kissed me, her hands fisting in my shirt to pull me closer. The kiss was hungry, desperate, full of two weeks of careful restraint finally breaking free. I groaned against her mouth, my arms tightening around her as I deepened the kiss.

When we broke apart, both breathing hard, her eyes were dark with desire. "Take me to bed, Kye."

I didn't need to be asked twice. I swept her up in my arms, carrying her toward our bedroom as she laughed breathlessly, her arms winding around my neck. The afternoon sun streamed through our windows, painting everything in golden light as I laid her gently on our bed.

"We have all the time in the world," I murmured against her ear, my hands already working at the buttons of her shirt.

"Then don't waste it," she whispered back, her fingers finding the hem of my T-shirt. We quickly stripped out of our clothes.

I looked into her eyes as she watched me, her breathing shallow and quick. "You're so beautiful," I whispered against her lips before capturing them in a searing kiss. My hand slipped between her thighs and brushed against her throbbing clit, feeling her shudder in response.

She moaned into my mouth, grinding her hips against my hand. I pulled back slightly to look at her, taking in the flush on her cheeks and the desire burning in her eyes. "You're going to beg for it, aren't you?"

"Please, Kye," she breathed, her voice barely above a whisper, the flush in her cheeks even darker than before. "I can't wait anymore."

With that word of permission, I leaned over her, caging her beneath my body. My cock throbbed painfully as I leaned down to take one of her perfect nipples in my mouth, sucking hard while running my fingers along her wet pussy. She arched off the bed with a moan, begging for more.

"On your knees," I commanded softly, watching as she obeyed without hesitation. I positioned myself behind her, running my rough hands along the lines of her body before gripping her hair tightly and pulling back her head. "Look at me," I growled into her ear, enjoying the shudder that ran through her at my dominance.

She met my gaze without flinching, her eyes dark with need. "Please, Kye. Don't hold back."

Without another word, I thrust myself inside her from behind, filling her up completely and claiming her as mine. She cried out in pleasure at the forcefulness of my entry but didn't protest. Instead, she pushed back against me and moaned louder as I began to pound into her from behind.

"You're mine," I grunted out between harsh breaths as I held onto her hips roughly and pumped myself deeper inside of her with each thrust. She responded by calling out my name like a prayer while we fucked furiously. Our bodies slid together in a rhythm neither of us could deny as sweat beaded on our skin and our hearts raced in unison. And when she came apart underneath me, I followed right after.

* * *

I woke to sunlight filtering through the curtains, painting warm stripes across our tangled bodies. Yulia slept peacefully in my arms, her hair spilling across my chest, her breathing deep and even. This wasn't the first morning I'd woken with her beside me, but it was the first where I didn't have to worry about our teenage daughter coming in, or someone calling to ask for something. The entire club had given us space.

I studied her face in the golden light -- the softness that sleep brought to her features, the dark sweep of her lashes against her cheeks. The memories of her kidnapping still lurked at the edges of my mind, but they seemed more distant this morning, pushed back by the warm weight of her body against mine, the certainty of her safety in my arms.

Her eyes fluttered open, blue and deep as the sky outside our window. For a moment, confusion clouded them -- the same momentary disorientation I'd seen during those first days after the rescue. Then recognition dawned, followed by a slow, sleepy smile that hit me straight in the chest.

"Good morning," she murmured, her accent thicker with sleep, the sound warming me from the inside out.

"Morning," I replied, my voice rough as I brushed a strand of hair from her face. "Sleep well?"

She nodded, stretching slightly against me like a contented cat. I pressed a kiss to her forehead, unable to find words for the emotions surging through me. She seemed to understand, her hand coming up to rest against my jaw, thumb stroking along the stubble there.

"Clover doing okay?" she asked, referring to our daughter's overnight stay with Cyclops and his family.

"Beast texted at some point last night saying she was all settled. I guess Cyclops hadn't wanted to bother us, but the Pres had a feeling we'd want to know how our girl was doing. Said Cyclops's daughter is thrilled to have her there." I smiled, picturing Clover, an only child, suddenly surrounded by three other kids. "They're planning to take everyone to town for lunch."

Yulia nodded, satisfaction evident in her expression. "Good. She deserves some normal teenage fun after everything."

She sat up slowly, the sheet falling away to reveal the bare curve of her shoulder, the delicate line of her collarbone. I watched, transfixed, as she slid from the bed and padded across the room to where my T-shirt lay discarded on the floor. She pulled it over her head, the fabric swallowing her smaller frame, hanging to mid-thigh in a way that somehow managed to be more enticing than full nudity.

Sunlight caught the ring on her left hand as she pulled her hair up into a messy bun, the pink diamond sending tiny reflections dancing across the wall. The sight of it -- that physical proof of our new reality -- sent a surge of possessive satisfaction through me.

She felt my gaze and looked up, catching me watching her. A faint blush colored her cheeks, but she didn't look away. "What?"

"Just enjoying the view," I said, allowing a smile to tug at my lips. "You in my shirt. Like something out of a dream."

Her blush deepened, but pleasure glinted in her eyes. "Not a dream anymore."

"No," I agreed, voice dropping lower. "Not anymore."

When she came back over to the bed, I shifted to make room for her. Instead of climbing back into bed, she stood beside it, staring down at me.

"We have the whole house to ourselves," she said, her voice taking on a husky quality I was quickly becoming addicted to. "All day."

"That we do." I reached for her, fingers hooking into the hem of my shirt where it hung at her thighs. "Any ideas how to pass the time?"

She caught my hand, but instead of pulling away, she used it to guide me to the bare skin beneath the shirt. "One or two," she admitted, the playfulness in her tone mixing with something darker, more urgent.

I tugged gently, pulling her back onto the bed and into my arms in one fluid motion. She came willingly, settling across my lap, her smaller frame fitting against mine like she'd been made for me. My hands found her waist, slid beneath the shirt to trace the curve of her spine, marveling at the softness of her skin beneath my callused fingers.

"God, you're beautiful," I murmured against her neck, tracing a path of kisses from her shoulder to her jaw. "Every inch of you."

She shivered under my touch, her head falling back to give me better access. Her fingers threaded through my hair, guiding me where she wanted me, newfound confidence in her movements that thrilled me to my core. Last night had been urgent, passionate -- the breaking of a dam after not only years of restraint but also being careful of her injuries the past few weeks. This morning was different, slower, more deliberate. We had time now. All the time in the world.

I pulled back enough to help her remove the shirt, leaving her gloriously naked in the morning light. The contrast between us was stark -- her pale, delicate frame against my larger, heavily tattooed body. Ink crawled up my arms, across my chest, telling the story of my life in the club. Her skin was unmarked save for the yellowing bruises from her ordeal and the silvery scars on her wrists from years ago -- reminders of her own journey, her own survival.

I lowered her carefully onto the mattress, hovering above her, supporting my weight on my forearms. My thumb traced the outline of the bandage still wrapped around her ribs, a physical reminder of how close I'd come to losing her.

Her hands sliding up my arms to my shoulders, pulling me down to her. When our lips met, it was like coming home -- familiar yet still new enough to send electricity racing through my veins. I took my time exploring her body, learning what made her gasp, what made her arch against me, what made her whisper my name like a prayer.

Even though she'd healed, I still worried I might hurt her. My touch became featherlight, gentler than I'd ever been with anyone, treating her like the precious thing she was.

"Okay?" I asked, watching her face carefully.

"Perfect," she breathed, the tension leaving her body as I continued my careful exploration.

When I slid inside her, it was with a slowness that bordered on reverence. I whispered her name against her skin, promises spilling from my lips that I'd never thought I'd say to anyone. Forever. Always. Mine. She answered with words in Russian -- endearments I didn't need to translate to understand, their meaning clear in the way her body moved with mine, the trust in her eyes as they held my gaze.

"I love you," I told her as we moved together, the words so long contained now flowing freely. "I love you, Yulia."

"I love you, Kye."

She came apart in my arms with a soft cry, her body tightening around mine, drawing me over the edge with her. I buried my face in her neck, overwhelmed by the intensity of it -- not just the physical release, but the emotional one. Years of wanting, of holding back, of telling myself the arrangement was enough -- all of it washed away in this moment of perfect connection.

Afterward, we lay tangled together, her head on my chest, my arm curved protectively around her shoulders.

"We should probably get up eventually," Yulia murmured against my skin, though she made no move to leave the warm nest of our bed.

I tightened my hold on her, pressing a kiss to the top of her head. "Eventually," I agreed. "But not yet."

Not yet. We had time now. All the time in the world.

We lay in comfortable silence, my fingers tracing idle patterns on Yulia's bare skin. The curve of her hip, the dip of her waist, the smooth expanse of her stomach. Her body was a map I was learning by heart, every scar and freckle a landmark to memorize. The morning had stretched into afternoon, but neither of us seemed inclined to leave our sanctuary. The world outside, with its demands and dangers, could wait a little longer.

Yulia's breathing had slowed to a peaceful rhythm, her body relaxed against mine. The sunlight had shifted, painting new patterns across the rumpled sheets. In these quiet moments, my mind wandered to possibilities I'd never allowed myself to consider before -- a future not just of survival, but of building something new together.

"Have you ever thought about having a baby?" The question slipped out before I'd fully formed it in my mind, born from the contentment spreading through me like warm honey.

The change in Yulia was immediate and visceral. Her body, seconds ago soft and pliant against mine, went rigid. She pulled away slightly, not enough to break contact but enough to create distance between us. When I looked down at her face, the color had drained from her cheeks, leaving her pale as bone china. Her eyes, which had been warm and languid with afterglow, now darted away from mine, fixing on some point across the room.

"Yulia?" I pushed up on one elbow, concern threading through me at her reaction. "What is it?"

She sat up fully then, drawing the sheet around her like armor, her slender fingers clutching the fabric so tightly her knuckles turned white. Several long seconds passed, the silence between us growing heavier with each tick of the bedside clock.

"I can't," she finally said, the words barely audible. "I can't have children."

The simple statement hung in the air between us, loaded with implications I couldn't immediately process. I sat up beside her, careful not to touch her yet, sensing her need for space.

"Can't?" I repeated, trying to understand.

Her hands trembled visibly now, and her breathing had grown shallow, almost panting. She still wouldn't meet my eyes, her gaze fixed on her own hands as they twisted the sheet into knots.

"Before they sent me to the boarding school," she began, each word seemingly dragged from somewhere deep and painful, "the Bratva... they made sure I would never..." She swallowed hard, her throat working against emotions that threatened to overwhelm her. "They were doing their best to wipe out my family's bloodline. If my sister hadn't managed to get away, they'd have done the same to her."

The meaning of her words hit me like a physical blow to the chest, momentarily robbing me of breath. Horror, then rage, then a grief so profound it had no name surged through me in rapid succession. Rage won out first -- white-hot and vicious, directed at people I'd never met but suddenly wanted to destroy with my bare hands. Men who'd taken a young girl -- a child -- and violated her in the most fundamental way possible.

"Jesus Christ, Yulia." My voice came out rougher than intended, and I saw her flinch slightly at the intensity. I took a deliberate breath, tamping down the fury that would only make this harder for her. "Who --

"

"It doesn't matter who," she interrupted, still not looking at me. "It was a long time ago. Before you found me."

The rage subsided, replaced by an ache that seemed to emanate from my very bones. This explained so much -- her nightmares in those early years, the way she'd flinched at sudden movements. I'd attributed it all to the trauma at the boarding school, never suspecting there had been earlier, deeper wounds.

"Why didn't you tell me?" I asked softly, no accusation in the question, just a need to understand.

"It wasn't relevant to our arrangement," she answered, a hint of the old formality creeping back into her voice -- a defense mechanism I recognized. "And later… I was afraid."

"Afraid of what?"

Her eyes finally met mine, swimming with unshed tears. "That it would change how you saw me. That it would matter once we…" She gestured vaguely between us, indicating our new relationship.

The protective instinct that had defined my feelings for her from the beginning surged forward, overwhelming everything else. I reached for her slowly, telegraphing my movements, giving her every opportunity to pull away. When she didn't, I gathered her gently into my arms, sheet and all, cradling her against my chest.

"Nothing changes how I see you," I told her, pressing my lips to the top of her head. "Nothing."

Her body remained tense within my embrace. "But what about children? You've been such a good father to Clover. Don't you want more kids? Your own biological children?"

The question made me pause, forcing me to examine feelings I hadn't fully explored. I'd never specifically thought about having more children -- my focus had always been on Clover, on the club, on keeping Yulia safe. But the idea that the choice had been violently taken from her, from us, before we'd even met… that cut deeper than I'd expected.

"I have everything I need," I finally said, the words simple but absolutely true. "You and Clover -- you're my family. That's all that matters to me."

She pulled back enough to search my face, looking for any sign of insincerity or disappointment. "I feel like I've failed you," she whispered, her voice breaking. "What if it causes problems later? What if you change your mind?"

I cupped her face between my hands, forcing her to hold my gaze. "Listen to me. You haven't failed anyone. You survived. You built a life. You've been an amazing mother to Clover." I brushed away a tear that had escaped to track down her cheek. "And I'm not going to change my mind about you. Ever."

The certainty in my voice seemed to reach her, some of the tension leaving her shoulders. She leaned forward, resting her forehead against mine, her eyes closing briefly.

"We'll face whatever comes together," I promised her, my thumbs stroking gently along her cheekbones. "Just like we always have."

She nodded slightly, not fully convinced perhaps, but willing to try. I eased us both back down onto the mattress, keeping her wrapped securely in my arms, her head tucked beneath my chin. We lay like that for a long time, not speaking, just breathing together. Her body gradually relaxed against mine again, though I could feel her mind still working, processing what this revelation meant for us.

My own thoughts churned beneath the surface calm. There was grief there, unexpected but real -- not for myself, but for her, for what had been taken from her without consent or warning. For the choices stolen before she was old enough to understand what they meant. And yes, perhaps a small mourning for possibilities that would never be. But alongside that grief was a bone-deep certainty that she was enough. She had always been enough.

The afternoon sun continued its slow journey across our bed, indifferent to the secrets we'd shared, the wounds we'd exposed. And through it all, we held each other -- bodies intertwined, hearts beating in sync -- processing in silence what it meant to build a future on foundations that had been altered before we'd ever met.

Chapter Thirteen

Salvation

I steered the truck around another bend in the forest road, the tires crunching over fallen pine needles and gravel. Beside me, Yulia gazed out the window, her profile softened by the dappled sunlight filtering through the trees. In the rearview mirror, I caught glimpses of Clover in the back seat, headphones on, her fingers tapping against her knee to some silent rhythm. My family.

"How much farther?" Yulia asked, her accent slightly more pronounced in the quiet of the truck cabin. Her left hand rested on her thigh, the rose-gold ring catching light every time we passed through a break in the canopy.

"About ten minutes," I said, reaching over to cover her hand with mine. "The turn-off is easy to miss. Beast said to look for the lightning-struck pine just past mile marker sixteen."

Yulia's fingers curled around mine, the simple contact sending warmth up my arm. After eleven years of careful distance, these casual touches still felt new, almost illicit -- a pleasure I was only beginning to allow myself.

Clover tugged her headphones down around her neck, leaning forward between our seats. "Is it really right on the lake? Beast didn't just say that to make it sound better?"

I glanced at her in the mirror, taking in the excitement that had replaced the shadows in her eyes. The kidnapping had left its mark on her -- nightmares, a new wariness -- but moments like this, when she looked like any normal teenager, eased the constant ache of guilt I carried.

"Right on the water," I confirmed. "Private dock and everything. Beast said they acquired it a few months ago for private getaways for the club families, but mostly it sits empty."

"Awesome!" Clover's enthusiasm made both Yulia and me smile. "I call the bedroom with the best view."

The road narrowed further, tree branches scraping occasionally against the truck's roof. We were deep in the forest now, far from the compound, from club business, from the world that constantly demanded pieces of me. Just us three, for three whole days. The weight that permanently lived between my shoulder blades began to ease, muscle by muscle.

"There." Yulia pointed to a massive pine split down the middle, its trunk blackened by an old lightning strike. "The turn-off."

I slowed the truck, carefully navigating onto what was little more than a dirt track. The suspension groaned in protest as we bounced over exposed roots and small rocks. Through breaks in the trees, I caught glimpses of water -- sunlight dancing across the surface of the lake like scattered diamonds.

The cabin appeared suddenly as we rounded a final bend, the forest opening up to reveal a clearing by the lakeshore. It was exactly as Beast had described -- rustic but solid, with weathered wooden walls and a wide porch that wrapped around two sides. A stone chimney rose from the pitched roof, and large windows faced the water, promising views from inside.

"It's perfect," Yulia breathed, her eyes taking in the peaceful setting. I watched her shoulders drop slightly, tension I hadn't even realized she was carrying visibly draining away.

I parked near the steps leading to the porch and cut the engine. The sudden silence was profound -- no motorcycles, no shouted conversations, no constant activity of the compound. Just birdsong, the gentle lap of water against the shore, and the whisper of wind through pine needles.

Before I could open my door, Clover had already leapt from the back seat, racing toward the cabin with the boundless energy of youth. "Can I look inside? Is it unlocked?"

"Key's under the mat," I called after her, unable to keep the smile from my voice. "Security system code is 0824."

Yulia and I climbed out more slowly, stretching limbs stiff from the three-hour drive. I moved to the truck bed, starting to unload our bags, but paused when I noticed Yulia standing motionless, her face tilted up toward the sun, eyes closed.

"You okay?" I asked, studying the planes of her face, the curve of her throat.

She opened her eyes, meeting mine with a softness I was still getting used to seeing directed at me. "Better than okay," she said.

I understood completely. The past weeks had been a whirlwind of emotions and adjustments -- our new relationship, Clover's enthusiastic acceptance, the club's knowing looks and occasional crude jokes. Every moment had felt observed, commented on, part of the communal life we lived. This was our first chance to just be us. A family.

"Dad! Mom!" Clover's voice rang out from inside the cabin, stumbling slightly over the new name she was still getting used to. "This place is amazing!

There's a loft with a skylight!"

Yulia's eyes brightened at the word "Mom," the simple syllable still new enough to bring a flush to her cheeks. I caught her hand, squeezing gently, understanding without words passing between us.

"You go on in," I said. "I'll get the bags."

She nodded but surprised me by rising on tiptoes to press a quick kiss to my lips before heading toward the cabin. I watched her walk away, still marveling at how different everything felt now. The same woman I'd lived with for eleven years but suddenly transformed by the simple acknowledgment of what had been building between us for so long.

I grabbed our duffel bags and two grocery sacks, muscles bunching under the weight. Inside, the cabin was just as impressive as the exterior had promised -- open-plan living area with exposed beams, a stone fireplace dominating one wall, comfortable-looking furniture arranged to take advantage of the lake view through floor-to-ceiling windows.

Clover had already disappeared, her excited voice echoing from somewhere upstairs. Yulia stood in the center of the main room, turning slowly to take it all in.

"Beast said they keep it stocked with basics," I said, dropping the bags near the sofa. "But I figured we'd want our own stuff too."

I carried the groceries to the small but well-appointed kitchen, Yulia following behind me. We fell into a familiar rhythm, unpacking and storing food side by side. When our hands brushed as we both reached for the same cabinet, neither of us pulled away. Instead, her fingers lingered against mine, a small smile playing at the corners of her mouth.

"This feels different," she said softly, voice

pitched just for me. "Being away from everything."

"Good different?" I asked, though I could read the answer in her relaxed posture, the absence of the vigilant awareness that usually accompanied her every movement.

"The best different," she confirmed, her accent wrapping around the words like warm honey.

I allowed myself to really look at her then. Her blonde hair hung loose around her shoulders, free from its usual practical ponytail. The bruises from her ordeal had faded completely, leaving her skin pale and perfect in the afternoon light. Her blue eyes held mine without the careful avoidance that had defined our interactions for so long.

"I love you," I said simply, because I could now. Because the words no longer had to be swallowed back, hidden away, denied.

Her smile widened, and she leaned into me, her body fitting against mine like it had always belonged there. "I love you too," she whispered against my chest.

Upstairs, Clover's footsteps thundered across the ceiling, followed by her voice calling down, "There's a canoe in the boathouse! Can we take it out later?"

Reality intruded, but gently, reminding us we weren't alone. "Tomorrow morning," I called back, reluctantly releasing Yulia to continue unpacking.

As I worked, I felt something unfamiliar settle into my bones -- a sense of rightness, of pieces clicking into place. For the first time in longer than I could remember, I wasn't a member of the Reckless Kings first and a man second. Here, I was just a father and a husband, spending time with his family in a peaceful place. And somehow, that felt like enough.

* * *

The forest trail wound around the edge of the lake, narrow but well-maintained, dappled sunlight filtering through the canopy overhead. I led the way, my footsteps instinctively quiet despite the peaceful surroundings, old habits impossible to break completely. Behind me, Clover chattered excitedly, stopping every few yards to examine something new -- a uniquely shaped rock, an interesting insect, the tracks of some small animal pressed into the soft earth. Yulia brought up the rear, her pace leisurely, hair loose around her shoulders. Away from the compound, she looked younger somehow, the vigilant awareness that normally characterized her movements replaced by a gentle ease that made my chest tighten with emotion.

"Dad, what kind of bird is that?" Clover pointed upward, where a flash of blue darted between branches.

"Blue jay," I answered, scanning the trees automatically for any sign of actual threat, finding none. "Noisy bastards, but pretty."

"Language," Yulia chided, but her smile took any sting from the admonishment.

I shrugged, unrepentant. "Just telling it like it is."

The trail curved sharply, and I held back a low-hanging branch for them to pass.

"Wait," I said suddenly, stopping in my tracks. I pointed toward a small clearing about thirty yards off the trail. "Look there. Don't move."

Clover and Yulia froze instantly, their bodies responding to the command in my voice before their minds could question it. A moment later, Clover's sharp intake of breath told me she'd spotted what I had -- a doe and two fawns, grazing peacefully in the dappled light.

"Oh," she breathed, barely audible. "They're

beautiful."

We stood motionless, watching the small family. The fawns stayed close to their mother, occasionally nudging at her side, tails flicking nervously. The doe kept her head up, alert, protective, even in this seemingly safe place. I understood that vigilance all too well.

"Just like us," Yulia murmured, so quietly I almost missed it.

We watched until the deer moved deeper into the forest, disappearing among the trees like ghosts. The moment broken, we continued along the trail, climbing steadily as it wound upward away from the shoreline. When the path grew steeper, roots creating natural steps in the incline, Yulia reached for Clover's hand without hesitation. My daughter -- nearly grown but still so young in many ways -- took it without the eye-rolling protest she might have shown back at the compound. Some walls came down here in the forest, away from watching eyes and reputations to maintain.

A hawk circled overhead as we crested a small rise, its wingspan impressive against the clear blue sky. I pointed it out to Clover, who tracked its lazy circles with fascination.

"Did they name Uncle Hawk after birds like that?" she asked, shielding her eyes against the sun.

I chuckled, the sound rusty but genuine. "Yeah. Story goes he could spot trouble from a mile away, like those birds spot prey. Nothing escaped his notice. Until he fell in love, then he screwed up in all kinds of ways before finally making Hayley his."

The trail opened suddenly into a clearing perched on a small rise above the lake. The view was spectacular -- water stretching to the distant shore, mountains rising beyond, the afternoon sun turning everything golden. A fire pit ringed with stones occupied the center of the clearing, clearly used by hikers before us.

"Perfect spot for a break," I announced, shrugging off my small backpack. "Think we can get a fire going before the sun drops too low?"

Clover's eyes lit up. "Marshmallows?"

I grinned, pulling a bag from the pack. "What's the point of a fire without them?"

While I arranged larger branches in the fire pit, Yulia and Clover gathered kindling from the surrounding forest edge. They worked together seamlessly, heads bent close as they discussed which sticks would burn best, Yulia pointing out particularly dry pieces, Clover darting to collect them. The sight of them together -- so similar in some ways despite no blood connection -- made something twist pleasantly in my chest.

Once the fire caught, flames licking eagerly at the dry wood, we settled around it in a tight semicircle. The breeze off the lake carried the clean scent of pine and water, mixing with the smokier smell of burning wood. I unwrapped the package of marshmallows, passing out long sticks I'd stripped of bark for roasting.

"The trick," I told Clover seriously, "is to keep it just above the flames, not in them. Slow and steady."

"Says the man who burns his marshmallow every single time," Yulia teased, her accent wrapping around the words like silk.

"I like them charred," I protested, deliberately plunging my marshmallow directly into the flames until it caught fire.

Clover burst into laughter as I blew out the small inferno, leaving a blackened, smoking lump on the end of my stick. "Dad! That's disgusting!"

"Don't knock it until you've tried it," I said, popping the entire burnt mess into my mouth with exaggerated satisfaction.

Yulia's laugh joined Clover's -- a sound so rare and precious it momentarily stopped my breath. Her head tilted back, throat exposed, eyes crinkled at the corners, all reserve forgotten.

The sky began to deepen toward evening, gold giving way to the first hints of pink and orange. We roasted more marshmallows, sticky sweetness coating our fingers, sugar buzzing in our veins. Clover told a story about school that had Yulia laughing again, and I found myself simply watching them, memorizing the way firelight played across their faces, the easy comfort between them that had grown over eleven years together.

This, I realized, was what I'd been fighting for all along. Not just their safety, not just their survival, but their happiness. Their freedom to laugh without looking over their shoulders, to exist without fear shadowing every moment. For the first time since the kidnapping -- maybe for the first time ever -- I felt completely present, completely at peace.

"Mom, do you have a napkin or something?" Clover asked, examining her marshmallow-coated fingers with dismay. "I'm all sticky."

The word dropped casually from her lips, natural as breathing, but its effect on Yulia was immediate and profound. Her eyes widened, then shimmered with sudden moisture. She still hadn't adjusted to Clover calling her that, but it was clear how much she loved it.

"Here," she said, voice slightly husky as she handed Clover a tissue packet. "Use water from the bottle too. It helps with the stickiness."

Clover simply nodded her thanks and began cleaning her hands.

I reached across the small space between us, taking Yulia's hand in mine, squeezing gently. No words needed. We understood each other perfectly. Family. Not by blood, not by law, but by choice. By love. By the bonds forged through hardship and protection and quiet moments like this one, when the world narrowed to just the three of us, connected by something stronger than DNA could ever be.

"I have something for you both," I said, my voice rougher than I intended. "Something I've been holding onto for a while."

They turned to face me, curiosity replacing the contentment on their faces. I pulled the wooden box from my pocket, its surface smooth and dark with age. It had belonged to my grandfather, one of the few things I'd kept from my life before the club. Small but solid, its brass hinges polished by years of handling.

"What is it?" Clover asked, moving closer, her eyes fixed on the box.

I opened it carefully, revealing its contents nestled in dark velvet. Two necklaces lay side by side, identical in design -- delicate silver chains supporting small pendants engraved with roses. The roses looked the same as the ones adorning Yulia's wedding ring, the detail so fine you could count individual petals despite their size.

"They're beautiful," Yulia whispered.

I lifted the first necklace from its velvet bed, the silver catching fire in the sunset light. "One for each of you," I said, holding it out toward Clover. "Because you're both mine to protect. To cherish."

Clover reached for it with uncharacteristic gentleness, her fingers trembling slightly as she took the delicate chain. "The roses match Mom's ring," she said. Clover didn't hesitate, immediately fitting the chain around her neck. The small pendant settled against her collarbone, the silver bright against her skin. "Will you help me with the clasp?" she asked, turning to present her back to me.

I fastened it carefully, my larger fingers clumsy with the tiny mechanism. When it was secure, she turned back, one hand coming up to touch the pendant, her expression solemn in a way that made her look older than her years.

"Thank you, Dad," she said simply, but the words carried the weight of all we'd been through together -- her mother's death, the explosion that had scarred her, the recent kidnapping, all the years I'd raised her as my own despite no blood connection between us.

I nodded, throat too tight for words, and turned to Yulia. She stood perfectly still, watching us with eyes that shimmered in the fading light. I lifted the second necklace from the box, holding it out toward her.

"I will always protect you both," I said, my voice thick with emotion I no longer tried to hide. "No matter what happens, we're a family now. For real. No more arrangements, no more pretending, no more separate lives under one roof."

Yulia's fingers trembled visibly as she reached for the necklace, her eyes never leaving mine. "It's beautiful," she said again, but I knew she meant more than just the silver and engravings.

"Turn around," I said softly. "Let me put it on you."

She did, gathering her hair to one side to expose the nape of her neck. The simple trust in the gesture --

turning her back to me, allowing me close to such a vulnerable spot -- spoke volumes about how far we'd come. I stepped closer, the scent of her skin mixing with pine and clean mountain air as I draped the chain around her throat.

My fingers brushed against her skin as I worked the clasp, and I felt her slight shiver at the contact. When it was secured, I didn't step back immediately. Instead, I leaned forward and pressed my lips to the spot just below her ear, a kiss that was both tender and possessive. "You're mine," I whispered, the words meant only for her. "You've always been mine."

She turned in my arms, her face tilted up to mine, tears tracking silently down her cheeks. "And you've always been mine," she replied. "Even when neither of us could say it."

I pulled her against me, one arm circling her waist while the other reached for Clover, drawing her into our embrace. For a long moment, we stood like that -- three bodies pressed close, three hearts beating in rhythm, three lives intertwined by choice rather than circumstance.

When we finally separated, the sun was balanced on the edge of the horizon, its last rays painting the sky in vivid oranges and pinks. We turned to face it together, standing in a line at the edge of the outcropping. Yulia's hand found mine, her fingers lacing through mine with the easy familiarity of long-time lovers, though we'd only crossed that line weeks ago. On my other side, Clover leaned against my shoulder, no longer trying to maintain teenage independence, just accepting the comfort of family. The pendant gleamed against Yulia's throat as she turned her face up to the blazing sky, a small smile playing at the corners of her mouth. Her other hand came up to touch it, fingers tracing the rose engraving in a gesture that mirrored how she often touched her wedding ring -- as if reassuring herself it was real, that this was real.

"Thank you," she said softly, the words carrying on the evening breeze. "For everything."

I understood what she meant. For saving her from her father's enemies eleven years ago. For giving her a home, a family, when she had nothing. For the years of respect and distance when she needed it. For finally finding the courage to cross that distance when we both were ready.

"Thank you," I replied, meaning just as many things. For helping raise my daughter. For standing by me through club business and violence and the life I'd chosen. For waiting until I was ready to admit what she meant to me. For loving me despite knowing exactly what I was capable of.

The sun slipped below the horizon, its last rays reaching across the lake like fingers of fire. In that moment, with Yulia on one side and Clover on the other, their matching pendants catching the fading light, I felt something I'd never experienced before -- a perfect, complete peace. Not just the absence of danger or the temporary quiet between threats, but a bone-deep certainty that I was exactly where I belonged, with exactly who I belonged with.

For a man who had lived his entire adult life in a world of violence and uncertainty, this feeling was as foreign as it was precious. I held onto it fiercely, memorizing every detail -- the weight of Clover against my side, the pressure of Yulia's fingers intertwined with mine, the scent of pine and lake water, the last gold light fading from the sky.

My family. Complete at last.

Harley Wylde

Harley Wylde is an accomplished author known for her captivating MC Romances. With an unwavering commitment to sensual storytelling, Wylde immerses her readers in an exciting world of fierce men and irresistible women. Her works exude passion, danger, and gritty realism, while still managing to end on a satisfying note each time.

When not crafting her tales, Wylde spends her time brainstorming new plotlines, indulging in a hot cup of Starbucks, or delving into a good book. She has a particular affinity for supernatural horror literature and movies. Visit Wylde's website to learn more about her works and upcoming events, and don't forget to sign up for her newsletter to receive exclusive discounts and other exciting perks.

Harley at Changeling: changelingpress.com/harley-wylde-a-196

Bad Boys Multiverse

Contemporary MC, Organized Crime, and Crossovers

- A Bad Boy Romance
- Dixie Reapers MC
- Devil's Boneyard MC
- Hades Abyss MC
- Devil's Fury MC
- Reckless Kings MC
- Savage Raptors MC
- Swift Angels MC
- Owned by the Mob
- Bryson Corners
- Underland MC

Paranormal MC

- Devoted Guardians MC
- Balor's Saints MC

Print and Audio:

- Dixie Reapers MC Print
- Dixie Reapers MC Audio
- Devil's Boneyard MC Audio
- Hades Abyss MC Audio
- Devil's Fury MC Audio

Changeling Press LLC

Contemporary Action Adventure, Sci-Fi, Steampunk, Dark Fantasy, Urban Fantasy, Paranormal, and BDSM Romance available in e-book, audio, and print format at ChangelingPress.com – MC Romance, Werewolves, Vampires, Dragons, Shapeshifters and Horror -- Tales from the edge of your imagination.

Where can I get Changeling Press Books?

Changeling Press e-books are available at ChangelingPress.com, Amazon, Apple Books, Barnes & Noble, Kobo, Smashwords, and other online retailers, including Everand Subscription and Kobo Subscription Services. Print books are available at Amazon, Barnes and Noble, and by ISBN special order through your local bookstores.

ChangelingPress.com

www.ingramcontent.com/pod-product-compliance
Lightning Source LLC
LaVergne TN
LVHW050641100826
845148LV00011B/1935